In the remote Dorset village of East Chaldon, T. F. POWYS (1875-1953) wrote a steady succession of novels, novellas, fables and short stories which first appeared in print during the 1920's and early 1930's. These tales of startling originality and strange beauty offer wry observations on the human condition, the enigma of God, and arresting insights into the nature of good and evil, infused with subtle and dark humour of the rarest vintage.

GH00503327

GLEN CAVALIERO, Fellow Commoner of St. Catherine's College, Cambridge, is a noted poet and critic. Among his books are *The Supernatural and English Fiction* (1995), *The Alchemy of Laughter* (2000) and *Charles Williams: Poet of Theology* (reissued, 2007). His most recent collection of poems is *The Justice of the Night* (2007).

Also available from The Sundial Press

UNCLAY by T.F. Powys

DURDLE DOOR TO DARTMOOR by Llewelyn Powys

STILL BLUE BEAUTY by Llewelyn Powys

THE BLACKTHORN WINTER by Philippa Powys

HESTER CRADDOCK by Alyse Gregory

KINDNESS IN
A CORNER

T. F. POWYS

THE SUNDIAL PRESS
2008

Kindness in a Corner was first published by
Chatto and Windus in 1930

This edition is published by The Sundial Press
46 The Sheeplands, Sherborne, Dorset DT9 4BS
www.sundialpress.co.uk

ISBN 0-9551523-5-6   ISBN 978-0-9551523-5-1

Printed by Biddles Ltd, Kings Lynn, Norfolk

CONTENTS

Introduction

Theodore Francis Powys (1875-1953) was one of three West Country brothers whose numerous books made the family name well known during the inter-war years. Unlike his elder and younger brothers, John Cowper and Llewelyn, he was known exclusively as a writer of fiction, in his lifetime publishing eight full-length novels and well over a hundred novellas and short stories. While living in a remote Dorset village he was to enjoy a certain vogue in the nineteen-twenties, thanks in part to the good offices of his friends David Garnett and Sylvia Townsend Warner; and his work was later to be championed in the academic world by the influential Cambridge critic F. R. Leavis. But with the possible exception of *Mr Weston's Good Wine* (1927) his novels have never reached a wide public, so that this reprint of its immediate successor is all the more to be welcomed.

Kindness in a Corner (1930) is among the most purely enjoyable of T. F. Powys's books and is thus a good introduction to its author's rustic world. On the face of it a quaint and mannered piece of amiable literary whimsy full of touches of light satire, it introduces us to an absent-minded scholarly bachelor clergyman, devoted to his books, to his armchair, and to his dinner, a man who lives in a benevolent tranquillity cared for by a tactful housekeeper and protected by the resourceful sexton, Mr Truggin. The setting is the village of Tadnol and the author provides Mr Dottery's parishioners with dialogue in the picturesque tradition already familiar from the novels of Thomas Hardy; and the narrative proceeds through simple statements of fact, authorial rejections and apothegms of a tendentious nature – altogether a relaxing literary methodology. The scene conjured up is just such a one as the more acidulous imagination of M. R. James had already subjected to invasions of a malign and preternatural character, and the Reverend Silas Dottery seems clearly marked out for disturbance in his serene and comfy corner. But the disturbances turn out to be of a humorous and farcical character rather than of a disabling kind.

Working in the literary tradition both pilloried and immortalised by Stella Gibbons's *Cold Comfort Farm* (1932), T. F. Powys had, in his early work especially, subjected his readers to a harsh portrayal of rural brutalities. *Mr Tasker's Gods* (1925), for example, is written with a ferocity that challenges comparison with the contemporary short stories of Caradoc Evans, with their unflattering depiction of narrow-minded Welsh chapel congregations; but Powys's ferocity is unleashed on behalf of the economically exploited as much as it is of their hypocritical exploiters. For even in this, the most savage of his novels, his vision is coloured by the Christian teaching instilled in him by his parents – Charles Francis Powys, Vicar of Montacute in Somerset, and Mary Cowper Johnson, descendent of a family that numbered among its luminaries the poets William Cowper and John Donne. In Theodore a similar sensitivity to pain, an awareness of mortality, of natural injustice, human fears and greed, were the more pronounced for being offset by a belief in the self-authenticating power of selflessness and love. He is not a writer likely to appeal to those of an easy-going or hedonistic temperament; and for all its playfulness *Kindness in Corner* is a novel that deals in the profounder human issues.

Powys's previous books, most notably *Mark Only* (1924), *Innocent Birds* (1926) and *The Market Bell* (unpublished until 1991), preserve a decidedly uneasy balance between a sombre pessimism and a compensatory sense of the enduring incorruptibility of innocence; and in his two specifically allegorical novels *Mr Weston's Good Wine* and *Unclay* (1931) he effectively solved this literary problem by positing an actual embodiment of Divine Providence at work in a village community that could, as a necessary result, take on the role of a cosmos. It may be that *Mr Weston's Good Wine* is Powys's literary masterpiece; but in *Kindness in a Corner* the reader is aware of an author writing for his own pleasure in a more intimate and homely manner, not so much a man with a message as a man who has taken that message to heart and is acting up to it accordingly.

It must be said, however, that the plot – to the extent that there is a plot at all in the book – verges in places on the downright silly: Bishop Ashbourne's visit to Tadnol in disguise is clumsily managed. But naturalistic plausibility is not a determining factor in T. F. Powys's portrayal of his world, and the inherent artifice involved in writing fiction is something that he takes for granted. If in Tadnol he creates his one idyllic community, there is nothing sentimental or over-sweet in its depiction. The stories about Tadnol that one finds scattered across his various collections all partake of a good-natured and tolerant atmosphere – it is not a place like his Dodder or Madder, Norbury or Shelton, in which the worst is always liable to happen. The ghost of Saint Susanna which haunts the green is the village's presiding genius and becomes incarnate in the person of the endearing Lottie Truggin, in whose portrayal Powys's delight in female sexuality finds its happiest expression. It is Lottie who ushers Mr Dottery out of self-enclosure into contemplation of a world that sets him free.

Much of the book's humour springs from Powys's caustic treatment of the bigoted religiosity of the clergy, and still more of their women-folk. (One wonders if he was aware of that charming Victorian hand-book concerning the behaviour of clergy wives, the Reverend Francis Paget's *The Owlet of Owlstone Edge* (1852) – the odious Miss Pettifer might have benefited from its perusal). Powys's resort to farcicality is always at the expense of the pompous, the self-deluded and the unforgiving, of heartless wealthy gentlefolk and niggardly censorious busybodies. His amusement at the folly of their pretensions, however, is laced with scorn, and is liable to end with a savage pounce. The clergy in general come in for a good deal of attention in his fiction; but if he is scathing about the conduct of such monsters as Mr Bromby in *The Market Bell* it is because of his affection for saintly pastors like Mr Hayhoe in *The Only Penitent* or even for the well-meaning limitations of a Silas Dottery. His scrutiny of those in Holy Orders is motivated by a sense of precisely how sacred their profession, when properly exercised, could be.

But *Kindness in a Corner* would not be as satisfying as it is were it not to sound a deeper note beneath the gentle frivolities of the surface happenings. There is an appropriate irony in the fact that this most light-hearted of Powys's novels should contain his most eloquent expression of belief in the beneficence of death. The fact that it is the comical Mr Truggin who consoles and converts the timorous Mr and Mrs Turtle serves to connect the graveyard, that corner "where God be kindness" with the corner in which Mr Dottery has ensconced himself, one in which he asks

How can it be possible ... to hurt and torment one another as we do, when we are, as we all must be, in present view of utter destruction? And these poor Tadnol people, how can they be harmed by sitting in the autumn sunshine rather than by crouching in a pew, with their knees touching their chins?

And this writer's essentially religious attitude to life can be seen in the words that follow.

Doth not God Himself – so near goeth the countryman to His doings – chirp as a sparrow on a plough, or lie as an autumn leaf driven into quietude at the bottom of an empty wagon?

This awareness of the immanence of God in all that exists issues in the question regarding life and death as which is which? In human experience the one can only be conceived in terms of the other: for T. F. Powys death is a completion, not an interruption. Such a concept may be alien to more strenuous theological contentions, but it was a conclusion in which this lover of quietness came to believe, and seldom did he voice that belief more persuasively than in this most unassuming of his extraordinary novels.

Glen Cavaliero,
Cambridge, 2008

1 THE CONFIRMATION

THE REVEREND Silas Dottery, the Rector of Tadnol, arose refreshed one morning from a long and sound slumber, bathed his body, dressed himself with his usual care and patience, and, taking a clean handkerchief from the proper drawer, descended the stairs with one hand upon the banister, and walked with a steady and unfaltering step across the hall into the dining-room.

A religious man culls good advice wherever he can find it, but Mr Dottery was one of those who go to books first – because for him they were the surest teachers and proved counsellors – and he had not so far sought in the stones, in the woods, or in a girl's laughter for sermons.

Mr Dottery had in his mind, as he made the journey from the bed-room to the dining-room – an important move to a good man – certain lines of Lucan that show the futility of being troubled about future evils.

Mr Dottery had pondered upon these thoughts of the Roman poet as he rubbed his wet beard with a heavy bath-towel. He had remembered them because Mrs Taste, the Rectory housekeeper, had observed – when she bid her master good-night the evening before – that she expected John Card, who was a sweep as well as a carter, to clean the kitchen chimney the next morning.

'It must have been,' thought Mr Dottery, 'such an evil as the coming of a sweep – rather than an executioner – into a gentleman's house that inspired Lucan to express himself so wisely, for a little troublesome thing may often prepare a man's mind to face bravely sterner evils.'

1

Though the evil was but the sweeping of the kitchen chimney – the study one was to escape this time – it might lead to other inconveniences, 'for would,' wondered Mr Dottery, as he sat now at his breakfast, 'would the state of this kitchen chimney that had hid and harboured so much soot – for Mrs Taste had said that it was very dirty – prevent the two plump grouse that were hanging in the larder safe from being roasted for lunch?'

Mr Dottery was not a man who understood hard manual labour – he had never been to prison – and, as he took all things easily himself, for he had a powerful mind that mastered his trade, so he believed that no one else had need to hurry over what he did. The sweep, he thought, would loiter over his own breakfast, just as he himself was loitering, and would arrive at the Rectory at about noon. 'Alas! then the birds must be kept for dinner.'

Mr Dottery stroked his beard. He expected some such disappointment. Every morning, and at each breakfast-time, there was always something or other that just set the balance right in his mind between a deep dejection of spirits and a too dangerous elation. For neither the one state nor the other accords with the right position of a man whose first parents fell, and whose careful humility can never be sure that all his sins will sink for ever in God's mercy.

The fat birds had been sent to Mr Dottery as a present.

To eat some crisp toast, with pure country butter – as naturally yellow as good butter should be – and an egg boiled the correct time, as set by Pope Innocent III – for exactly three minutes and a half and timed by a sure glass – and then a little more toast and butter with a spoonful of Oxford marmalade, always occupied a decent half-hour of

Mr Dottery's morning. And he never failed to smile a little as he ate of the last dish – as a loyal Cambridge man should – and murmur into his cup:

'They think themselves scholars there, but they know that all they can really do well, under those green-muffled Cumnor hills, is to make a sweetmeat.'

After slowly drinking his third cup of coffee – for he never took less, liking the number three – into which he had poured a liberal allowance of rich cream, Mr Dottery rose from his chair, and going to the window, that was wide open, he leaned out of it.

The season was summer, the month August, and a young and tender vine that had been planted below the window, well watered by the summer rains and warmed by the sun, showed a desire – as a green thing will – to creep into the Rectory dining-room to see what went on there.

Although Mr Dottery was not the kind of man to notice with any marked attention Nature's ordinary doings, yet he regarded this vine with considerable interest, wondering that anything so meek should grow so fast, and admiring its pertinacity in climbing so high without an invitation.

Mr Dottery plucked off the boldest tendril and remembered the sweep.

Mr Dottery honoured the king; under the king he honoured every good man, but he feared a sweep.

No one, he knew – not even the pilot of a ship, no, nor even Death himself – could enter any human habitation and so completely command there. Who would dare to oppose the entrance of a sweep, or dare to say the least word against the plans appointed by such an exacting person? Even the Centurion, who was so well obeyed by his servants, would never have ventured, Mr Dottery knew, to command a sweep.

Perhaps he was already come.

Mr Dottery went back to the table and took up the letter-bag that he had not yet unlocked. As he did so, he was aware that the drive gate had been opened, and that a large motor-car was moving up to the Rectory front door. Mr Dottery unlocked the letter-bag, and turned his head slightly, so that he was able to see two gentlemen leave the car and approach the door.

'The sweep and his assistant,' murmured Mr Dottery absentmindedly, and added, 'but, thank God, it's not the study chimney today!'

Mr Dottery opened his letters. There was nothing, he was glad to see, that needed to be answered. He might have the morning to himself – indeed, the whole day – for he could remember no engagement that could possibly interfere with his own studies. He looked forward to a quiet day, to a good, pious day with no interruptions, to a morning with his books, to a wholesome walk in the afternoon, and then to reading again.

Mr Dottery took up a silver paper-knife in order to cut the wrapper from *The Times*, for it was his custom to open the paper at breakfast time to learn if the king was in good health, or if any old friend of his were dead or married, and then to fold the paper again until after lunch.

After cutting the wrapper and unfolding the paper, he found the page wherein the king of England is always mentioned with rightful honour. Mr Dottery paused in his reading and laid down *The Times*. Mrs Taste had knocked at the door.

Mr Dottery bid her come in. He believed he knew what she had come to tell him.

'I am already aware,' he said, 'that the sweep has arrived, but I am sure I can depend upon you, Mrs Taste, to treat a tradesman, who is learned in so dark and hollow a mystery as the scouring of a chimney, with a proper hospitality. Pay him before he leaves, and while he is under our roof give him all that he asks for, but if he hints, however cunningly, about the study chimney, tell him that all is well there.'

While he spoke Mr Dottery had not looked at Mrs Taste, but when she did not reply to him he turned to her. Mr Dottery was surprised: Mrs Taste showed by her looks that she was very much frightened.

'He is not gone to the study already, I hope?' exclaimed Mr Dottery.

'They are both there,' replied Mrs Taste, trembling, 'Bishop Ashbourne and Canon Dibben.'

When once a good man, who knows the old writers, has received one little shock – such as the likelihood of his luncheon being but a cold one – a second trial, though of greater calibre than the first, does hardly move him. For the peace of mind when once disturbed by the explosion of a little squib can bear with equanimity, a few moments later, the roar of a great cannon.

Mr Dottery brushed a crumb from his lap.

'And their business, Mrs Taste?' he asked.

'The Confirmation,' she replied breathlessly.

Mr Dottery looked for another crumb, and blushed.

'The Confirmation is today,' said Mrs Taste.

Mr Dottery brushed his coat where no crumb was.

'I forgot all about it,' he said.

2 THE BISHOP'S SHILLING

'IT must have been the weather,' sighed Mr Dottery, 'for yester-day I had only walked about a mile toward Shelton when I was met by a thunder-shower that wetted me sadly, and when I returned home, I remembered to change my clothes, but forgot the Confirmation. But it's these newly-married gentlemen,' said Mr Dottery, more gaily, 'who should have forgotten it.'

Mr Dottery smiled. The newly-appointed Bishop of Portstown, a younger brother of the wealthy Dean Ashbourne, had, only a little while before, been married to his second wife, a spinster named Miss Agnes Pettifer. And, in the same paper in which he had read of this happy event, Mr Dottery had also seen the account of the wedding of Canon Dibben, the Vicar of Dodder, who had taken to wife a certain Miss Cockett at the same time and, indeed, at the same hour that Bishop Ashbourne and Miss Pettifer went to the altar.

'Those thunder-showers,' sighed Mr Dottery, 'they come so suddenly.'

'The Confirmation is at one o'clock,' said Mrs Taste.

'The Bishop and Canon Dibben are unduly early,' observed Mr Dottery. 'And it would have been more fitting had they met me at the church at the hour of the service. To call now is very inconvenient, when I have so short a time to prepare the candidates. Will you be so kind, Mrs Taste, as to request Truggin to attend me here?'

Mrs Taste withdrew, closing the dining-room door very silently, and went to give her message to Mr Truggin, the Rectory gardener, who was also the clerk and sexton of Tadnol Church. She had not to go far, for ever since eight o'clock had struck, the exact hour when a clear

6

brisk fire had been lit in the kitchen grate after the chimney had been swept, Truggin, who knew his master's fears, had been beside it, drinking strong ale in honour of the subtle Card, the high priest of the sooty festival. Mrs Taste came into the kitchen, and delivered her message.

Without waiting to reply to John Card, who had ventured timidly to observe that he believed, weather permitting, that the proper time had come for sowing the seeds of the greater variety of spring onion, Truggin rose to attend his master.

He was not altogether unlike him. He wore a beard as his master did. He took his pleasures soberly as a good church officer should – but he had also an opinion that was his own. He believed that all men and women have in their hearts, through all their foolishness, one decent wish – to be buried. And as he thought so, he also knew that he, Sexton Truggin, was the one to bury them.

When Truggin entered the dining-room, he found his master looking with interest at the little vine-shoot that he had plucked off and had laid beside his plate.

'Even such a green thing,' said Mr Dottery, as Truggin entered, 'was once carried by the faithful Dove home to the Ark when the waters were upon the earth.'

'And the sight of thik,' replied Truggin, 'did make Noah thirsty for wine.'

'The virtues of the vine were unknown to him,' said Mr Dottery,' or else he would have drunk more wisely.'

Mr Dottery moved back his chair and stretched.

'The Bishop has come,' he said, 'to hold the Confirmation here.'

'So I be told,' remarked Truggin.

'Then will you be so good,' said Mr Dottery, putting the vine leaf onto his plate, so that it might be taken away, 'as to ring the church bell, that all things may be ready for the service at a quarter to one. You will, if you please, neglect nothing at this Confirmation that should rightfully be done in honour of the Bishop's coming.'

'But what be 'en out to confirm?' asked Truggin.

Mr Dottery bowed his head a little, and touched his forehead with his hand as if to help his memory.

'He is here to confirm,' he said, 'all those that are placed ready, and stand in order before him.'

'Then 'e'll have to lay hands on fleas and spiders,' said Truggin, 'for all they maidens be gone to the fete at Shelton.'

Mr Dottery and his clerk looked at one another, not reproachfully, but merely to gain a little time to think what ought to be done, for both knew that both were to blame.

'I forgot the Confirmation,' said Mr Dottery sadly.

'And they maidens minded the fete,' said Truggin.

'But, surely,' said Mr Dottery, 'there must be one or two young women, of a suitable age to be confirmed, left in Tadnol?'

'Only me granddaughter, Lottie, who be thee's own servant,' replied Truggin, 'and she be crying and sobbing in bedroom.'

'And why?' inquired Mr Dottery.

'Because Mrs Taste do say,' answered Truggin, 'that sweep's days weren't fete days for servant maidens.'

'Nor for the clergy either,' observed Mr Dottery, with a groan, 'and yet I ought to be grateful to John Card, who today has been the means of giving a candidate for the Confirmation. Be so good, Truggin, as to retire and to inform Mrs Taste that I wish Lottie to dry her eyes and to come to me, so that I may prepare her for the service.'

A young girl is a deep mystery. When she enters a room something enters with her that belongs to the earth and to the sun, to the carnal and to the holy. A warm, earthy thing, a star of heaven. Pagan and yet merry with God, a presence that wishes to be kind, but opens a door to sorrow.

When Lottie Truggin, who was just seventeen years old, came into the Tadnol Rectory dining-room, Mr Dottery never looked at her, for he was busy turning over the leaves of a large prayer-book, in order to find the page he needed.

'Can you say the Creed, the Lord's Prayer, and the Ten Commandments?' he asked of her; 'and can you answer to such questions as in the short Catechism are contained?'

Lottie drew herself up to her full height, plumed herself like a robin, and put her hands behind her.

'Oh yes,' she answered proudly. 'I can say all that, and I can dance too, and ride a roundabout.'

'Then put on a white veil,' said her master gladly.

'But I haven't one,' replied Lottie, wiping her eyes that were still a little moist, 'for who would have expected the Bishop to come on the day of the Shelton fair?'

'Not I,' sighed Mr Dottery.

'No, nor none other of us,' said Lottie, 'for when 'twas given out in church that the Bishop was coming, there wasn't no day mentioned.'

'Alas!' murmured Mr Dottery, 'I must have omitted the date.'

''Tweren't all your fault,' said Lottie, 'for thee hadn't the fete to think of to remind thee of the day.'

'I am glad that you didn't go to Shelton,' said Mr Dottery, searching in the prayer-book for any other question that he ought to ask.

'Oh, but I wish I had,' said Lottie, giving a little sob.

Mr Dottery rang the bell.

'Be so kind,' he said, when Mrs Taste answered his call, 'as to lead this young woman away and to give her a white veil, for she has come to years of discretion, and it is proper that holy hands be laid upon her.'

As soon as Lottie was gone Mr Dottery considered for a few moments what he ought to do next, and then a little wearily, and taking long, slow strides, he went to the study. His visitors rose from their chairs to greet him.

'I congratulate you upon your marriage, my lord, and you too, Canon Dibben,' said Mr Dottery in a courtly manner, when he had bid his guests welcome.

Bishop Ashbourne was a small stout man, clean-shaven, with a merry eye, and a face inclined to roundness, together with a mouth that was a large one. The mouth looked hungry.

Mr Dibben was quite another matter. He was tall and as lean as a tom-cat, with a moustache that was like a cat's whiskers. His boots were trodden down at heels, and he looked always at the Bishop as at one who gives preferment in a smile.

In good courtly company one is not expected to talk of the matter in hand. At a funeral, where the proper people are gathered, one talks of the Russian poets or of a sort of little curly-haired dog. At a wedding

10

the conversation generally turns upon the growing of strawberries, or upon the first bicycle, that was called a bone-shaker.

Bishop Ashbourne began to talk of the harvest moon. But Canon Dibben looked at the clock.

'You will take a glass of wine and a biscuit before the service, gentlemen?' said Mr Dottery, with his hand upon the bell.

'Beer, if you please,' replied the Bishop, 'for I have had a very poor breakfast.'

Mr Dottery rang the bell, and in a few minutes refreshments were brought in.

'It's nearly time for the service,' observed Canon Dibben, 'and, in order that my lord may robe himself decently, we should soon be going to the church.'

The Bishop put down his glass, looked at the Canon, shook his head, filled his glass again from the jug, drank it off, brushed the biscuit crumbs from his apron, and rose to go.

In the church all was ready. The door had been unlocked, and Mrs Truggin, the wife of the clerk, had turned the cloth upon the altar – which she did whenever she thought the cloth looked dirty – and had also dusted the high-backed chair that she supposed the Bishop would use.

The bell stopped ringing, and the clergy entered, robed, from the vestry.

Bishop Ashbourne was a dutiful churchman. Whenever he entered the building, mockingly called 'a steeple house' by George Fox, it was prayerfully, as though he breathed the same air as God. Thinking so, he had no wish to see who else was there.

But Canon Dibben was not so modest. He looked down the church and saw no one.

'Where are the candidates?' he whispered to Mr Dottery.

Mr Dottery strode down the aisle, and looked here and there, until he was fortunate enough to discover Lottie Truggin hiding behind a pillar. Holding her by the hand, he led her to the altar-rails.

Lottie had no need to be nervous. She was covered by a splendid veil that Mrs Taste had made in ten minutes out of an old pair of drawing-room curtains.

Lottie stood reverently, and the service commenced.

One of the most striking virtues of a holy service done in a church is that the glamour of its consequence is neither lessened nor diminished by the fact that only two or three are gathered there. An empty church, where those two or three are, is no defaulter. A holy peace never wants company. And a good priest is never at a loss for a congregation; his prayers create a people.

Bishop Ashbourne was not aware that he laid his hand upon only one child, though Canon Dibben looked aggrieved.

The Bishop uttered the blessing: the service was over.

But, before the clergy withdrew to the vestry, Sexton Truggin approached them with a collecting-bag. Bishop Ashbourne gave a shilling.

In less than an hour that shilling purchased four rides upon a roundabout for Lottie Truggin at Shelton fair.

3   KITCHEN RULE

THE bones of an ancient monster can rest snug in the clay for two hundred millions of years without a change coming to them. And so one need not be surprised that a month or two can pass over the roof and the ivied walls of a country parsonage without anything happening within that is of much moment.

But when the month of October came to Tadnol, it seemed that something had happened there that did not accord with the ordinary daily progress of kindly doings, where everyone wished to please and to be pleased. 'Twas perhaps but a little thorn, one of those that lie about, hidden in a grassy bank, and scratch the hand of a girl who gathers the first snake-flower.

The Reverend Silas Dottery looked uncomfortable. What it was that made him look so, no one knew.

Lottie Truggin guessed at the cause. She was not one of those young women who go to the top of a mountain to find trouble when what is looked for is really at home. Lottie gave it as her opinion, because her master seemed a little strange, that he had the belly-ache, or was – to put the matter into the more genteel words of Samuel Richardson – 'a little out of order'.

Lottie liked to speak plainly, and as those she spoke to in the village listened to her and believed what she said, she made the same observation to Mrs Taste at supper, but received so stern a look from the housekeeper – though Mrs Taste had thought the same herself and had hinted darkly to her master about the virtues of camomile tea – that Lottie dared not open her mouth again that evening.

The October rooks, as well as Lottie, knew that something must be wrong in the little village that knelt so piously beside the river, for they flew wildly in the air to show their sympathy, as well as to tell one another that the winter storms might soon be expected, and that the fading leaves had better look to themselves, for the kingly rule of their high lord, the summer sun, was nigh over.

Though it is a rare thing, in these degenerate days, to find a kitchen in which kindness rules, yet there may perhaps be found others like our Tadnol, where the gardener kneels to weed the drive, where evil hath not entered, and where love and religion – those twin guardians of the peace of God – still rule.

A good kitchen is a home fit for the blessed saints, where all is warmth, comfort, and good victuals, and where two great warming-pans shine ever upon the walls like the cheeks of God. Those that rule there rejoice with the parlour company, and suffer with them too.

Indeed, they do more than suffer with them, for they try to soothe the unhappy with tender mutton and parsley sauce with capers. And, if that will not do, they try a clear soup, or a fish pudding that has no bones in it.

But though there be love in a kitchen and good fare, that the clever hand of a cook never neglects to set before the master, yet kitchen rule can be a very forceful tyrant.

The poor slave of this tyrant may pretend a gladness in the day and close his book to walk upon the hills. But he is soon reminded that, though loosed for a little, he is chained fast to a table, and, though he looks onwards, yet he has always a lingering wish to go backwards.

Aha! when once rich roasted flesh, well-baked in an oven that glows as a fiery furnace, be the matins and evensong, the sun, the moon and the stars do not fail to bow down before the steaming altar. The cool sweetness of the green fields is curdled by the odour of the hog's puddings; each pile of earth that is a hill and every flowery mead have a culinary look, and a scent as though mushrooms fry in butter.

About luncheon-time, in summer, when a man would lay the poor body of his flesh down upon a soft bank amongst the violets and look up at the changing colour of God's home, which is the sky, the fumes from his own chimney command him to return, and the kitchen king draws him indoors.

And doubtless many would wonder whether Tadnol had anything better to give than a well-cooked dinner with all the appurtenances thereof.

But there is the river with its rushes and water-flowers and sweetness and melancholy, the steep hill with its high hedges that leads up to the heath, where only lonely footsteps wander – they can free for a few hours at least a poor table slave ...

'I do mind,' said Lottie, as she took up a dish-clout to wipe the dinner-plates, 'that I was once forced to lie down flat on the floor after eating three helpings of apple-pie.'

Mrs Taste pretended not to hear her. She was thinking of the last time when Mr Dottery had seemed as worried, because there is nothing new under the sun.

She remembered the occasion. Mr Dottery's niece, Barbara, had misbehaved herself when in her teens, running to a young man in Paris on one day, and running away from him on the next. Her mother – a widow, and Mr Dottery's only sister – bid him come to London to chastise Barbara with scorpions. Mr Dottery had thought he ought to go. He passed three days in extreme agony. On the fourth day he turned over the pages of the *Saints' Everlasting Rest*, and sent Barbara a birthday present.

That had all happened because of a letter. If a letter could come once and take away the master's appetite – that was, upon the whole, remarkably good for a man of his years – a letter could come the second time and do the same mischief.

But perhaps Mr Dottery was going to be ill.

4 MR DOTTERY FORGETS THE WINE

A WOMAN who attends to the wants of a country scholar – a man who is often but a closed coffin for the dead languages – whether she be his wife, his daughter, or his cook, will always note with care the least symptom of uneasiness in her lord that may be the commencement of a serious illness. And, though the scholar generally is a very simple fellow, as mild as a dove and as fearful of any pain, yet he will not always behave, when pinched, just as one would expect.

There are various ways to express vexation, the most common being a settled and surly gloom that breaks out now and again into ugly bursts of temper – the symptoms of a hideous inner fear. But the behaviour of a troubled divine is likely to be different – as becomes one who dies daily to himself, who should be, and often is, schooled in quietude – so that the usual antagonism between the conflicting forces of doing much and suffering much is wanting in him.

Within his content in God, pain alone can set him a task – a simple one. 'Tis but a closing of doors, 'tis but a retirement, and never a battle. But even the closing of a door may make a little creak ...

Upon Mr Dottery's breakfast-table, and close to the gleaming coffee-pot, there was always placed a pretty cream-jug – that had been his mother's – which was filled full of rich cream. Nearby, there was also a plain white milk jug, of a virgin purity, though of the finest china, that contained milk.

The milk would be carried out, as it was carried in – a virgin, but the cream jug would be emptied.

17

When Mrs Taste first began to fear for Mr Dottery's health, the milk had been deflowered and the cream left untasted. Mrs Taste looked at the unused cream and then at Lottie Truggin.

Something, she knew – a dark cloud, as heavy as an uncooked suet pudding – musy be hanging about Tadnol Rectory, to foretell disaster.

Mrs Taste had not served a man for twenty-five years without learning a little about him, and the most alarming sing of all, in any man, is a change in his settled habits. A small error, putting the wrong foot upon the stairs first, some little odd in an even journey, she knew, might be the beginning of the end.

Mrs Taste said nothing, but she took down from the bookcase her great Bible, placed it upon the kitchen table, and waited till dinner-time.

Mr Dottery always brought up the wine himself, and decanted it through a silver funnel, with the utmost care so that he never spilt a drop, but that evening Mr Dottery forgot the wine!

Another portent came too, but this time from the garden tool-shed. There was thick mud upon Mr Dottery's boots! As he always chose the cleanest ways, this mud showed that, in taking his usual afternoon walk, he must have turned by mistake down Farmer Spenke's dirty lane.

Mr Truggin carried a boot, all muddy as it was, into the kitchen to show it to Mrs Taste.

Mud upon a boot can have a deep meaning. It can often tell a fine story of strange wanderings. If a man strays a little out of the way, mud will be upon him.

''Taint to be thought of,' said Truggin, 'that master did go down to the river to catch an eel.'

18

'They Spenke maidens be as wriggly,' observed Lottie.

Mr Truggin shook his head, and carried the boot away to clean it.

As Truggin cleaned the boot, he pondered over it. He loved his master, but he was a man who loved a grave too. Mrs Taste wished to preserve Mr Dottery and, by means of her excellent cooking, to give him a long life: Truggin wished to bury him.

'Twas a pleasant consolation to Truggin to cut the grass and daisies with a sharp spade, to open the earth and to take out the soil. He would dig slowly, for to him it was a holy pastime. He would dig lovingly, for he was performing an act of love. He was making a bed of joy that would remain until the end of the world. Those that Truggin loved, he wished to bury.

If Truggin had a belief it was in the holiness of a grave. The whole earth, he fancied, the vault of heaven, all the stars, could never have reached to so great a glory unless, somewhere or other – and at Tadnol better than elsewhere – there was a grave.

The sorrow of the earth could never be full so that it overflowed into joy, unless there was a grave in which tears might become pearls of goodly price. The stillness of a midsummer's night, with a heavy slumbering moon above, could never be so still unless in the church-yard a grave had been dug.

Although Truggin was sorry for his master, he was glad for himself. He had begun to dig the potatoes in the Rectory garden, which was a task that he always enjoyed. He liked the time of year – the autumn – when the damp winds began to shake the leaves off the churchyard trees. Truggin liked that. Nature always knew how to behave at the proper time, she knew how to shake anything down.

19

Nature, Truggin knew, was all-powerful and all-kind, but in heaven there dwelt One who was even kinder. Nature was but a sorry manager. She would leave what dies upon the surface of the earth, as though nothing matters anymore when life was extinguished.

But God knows better. He put into man's heart the love of dead things and the wish to bury them.

Truggin was a man who could enjoy himself. To him pleasure was profit, and profit pleasure. He never refused what was offered to him in a kindly way. The Tadnol burial fees were low, and yet, with one thing and another, Truggin was usually able to gain a pound sterling when a corpse was committed to the ground.

Truggin liked a man who looked at the ground in the right way. Mr Dottery always regarded the sod with a proper respect. But Canon Dibben did not do that. He looked at the earth – even in a churchyard – as if it were nothing of consequence, and only fit to be trod upon.

Canon Dibben, too, liked to see men busy, always working and making a noise, praying loudly or beating carpets.

Truggin, true to his own mystery and to Mr Dottery's sermons, believed that stillness and silence were the only supreme good and there was only one remedy for all the evils under the sun – a decent burial.

Mr Dibben thought differently. He never failed to open his mouth widely when he spoke, and to show his bad teeth. Mr Dibben believed in war and battle, in angry resistance, in making sin run. He believed that evil could be beaten out of a man and the sinner cleansed.

Though Canon Dibben was a man whose ways Truggin did not like, he once tried – in the most natural way for him – to do the Canon a good turn. He tried to bury him.

Canon Dibben was always one to pry about, in order to help – as he supposed he did – the Church of England. He had heard in his own village of Dodder – indeed, from his own wife – that Mr Dottery kept a concubine somewhere. A young girl had been seen praying on the green, whom no one knew, but Mr Dibben did not know that Saint Susanna haunted Tadnol – and he wished to save a sinner.

He chose a day to visit Tadnol when old Mother Spenke was lying dead, lamented by all – now that she was dead – and Truggin, who was always beforehand with this business, had dug her grave early and covered it with thin boards.

Mr Dibben wished to see the church, for although Mrs Dibben said that Mr Dottery kept his sin nearer home, yet Mr Dibben knew that in modern days – in which everything is so upside down – a harlot might prefer a church to powder herself in to a parlour.

Mr Dibben called at the sexton's for the key. Going into the church-yard, he walked on the grass. This displeased Truggin, who had no wish that his graves should be trampled on. Mr Dibben went on because he wanted to peep into the vestry window before entering the church. He knew that much could be done in a vestry. But Mr Dibben chose a dangerous path.

Right in his way, and between two old gravestones, was the new grave in which Mrs Spenke had not as yet taken up her abode.

Truggin turned aside, but Canon Dibben fell into the pit.

Whether the next thing that happened was Truggin's doing or Saint Susanna's, who can say? But a good barrow-load of earth from the heap nearby fell after Mr Dibben and buried him. Truggin shook his head over the Canon, who crawled out, half stifled, for he was afraid

21

that Dibben would surely be damned. Later Truggin said to his wife that if the clergyman had really had the grace of God in him, together with the repentant wish to do no more evil as an informer, he would have lain still, and remained there for ever.

'Then you must have dug another grave for Mrs Spenke,' observed Mrs Truggin.

'Have I ever refused to dig one?' cried Truggin.

'No,' replied his wife. 'Never!'

That night, in a dream, a curious idea came to Truggin. He dreamed that the village of Tadnol was a rabbit warren, that Death was the trapper, and that he, Truggin, was the fee'd helper.

'Listen,' he said to his granddaughter, Lottie, who had run home for a moment before breakfast, 'listen to they steps that be passing. 'Tis the old man who be out a-setting of his snares – a fine warren be Tadnol.'

5 'IT MAY PLEASE THEE
TO COMFORT AND RELIEVE THEM'

B ESIDES knowing the right way, and the right time – as often as they die – to bury a man, Truggin also understood money. He could add, he could subtract, he could divide money.

The money that Mr Dottery paid him and the money that he earned as gravedigger he would carry home in his hand and lay out upon the cottage table, and then he would set to work at his arithmetic. He would divide the money into two equal parts. One half he took to himself for beer, the other half he gave to his wife.

The idea of thus dividing his earnings came to Truggin one Easter Sunday in the church porch, when he handed the collecting-bag to Mr Dottery – having forgotten to do so before – and received, all as a gift, ten shillings. Mr Dottery, thinking of the going and coming of money, informed Truggin that King James the Second spent upon himself and upon his royal household – amongst whom he numbered Wycherley – one quarter of the whole revenue of the country.

Before Truggin had heard this news, it had been his custom to give the larger part of all that he earned to Mrs Truggin.

'But how much better,' he now said to his wife, 'to be a live sexton at Tadnol than a dead king in London.'

'One be meat and t'other be bones,' observed Mrs Truggin.

'And so,' exclaimed Mr Truggin, hitting the table with his fist, 'if they bones did take a quarter of all, 'tis right for I to take half.'

'Of what?' asked Mrs Truggin.

'Of me money,' replied her husband.

Mr Dottery would have been very much surprised had he been told that the people of Tadnol loved him. He had always hoped that he did them no harm. He was well aware, though, that no one knows the harm he does.

'Evil and Good are both veiled women,' he was wont to say, 'and it is very easy to mistake the one for the other.'

Mr Dottery never failed both at morning and at night to kneel down and say aloud a collect or prayer for all conditions of men, to be used at such times when the Litany is not appointed to be said. And when he came to the words, 'to all those distressed in mind, body, or estate,' he would say, 'and also the men, women, and children of this parish, only make not all thy ways known to them, but thy kind ways alone – and that it may please thee to comfort and relieve them ...'

Had Mrs Taste been God's housekeeper instead of Mr Dottery's – and there is every reason to believe that she will attain to such a dignity – she could not have done more to make God's best ways, fine gifts of puddings and pies, and wine that is a mixture, known to Tadnol.

Although not a rich man, Mr Dottery had enough and to spare. He believed that God gave gifts to Farmer Spenke – corn and milk and butter – and that he also gave gifts to Silas Dottery – an armful of pound-notes each year.

Many little birds fed of the farmer's corn, and many other birds fed at Mr Dottery's expense.

'God's mercy is infinite,' Mr Dottery would say in his sermons; 'He has no pleasure in a frown, He prefers to smile, and He likes nothing better than to give with both hands.'

The Tadnol people respected Mr Dottery; they also respected his manner of living, for he lived well.

To have business at the back door of the Tadnol Rectory about dinner-time was indeed a pleasure to a poor man, whose nose told him that good fare appeareth sometimes otherwise than in a dream.

All Tadnol knew that Mr Dottery took wine, and all Tadnol knew that the wine that Mr Dottery drank at dinner would have made Blacksmith Croot forget that he had ever shod a horse and remember that he had once sung a song.

A clergyman and his village will often try to stare one another out of countenance. Therefore a wise man who is in orders in the country will always provide something for the people to stare at, so that he may escape. A large black curly dog may be employed, or a stout wife who rides a bicycle. And Mr Dottery had, behind his house in a little lane, a heap of empty bottles, as high as a small haystack!

Mr Dottery stayed at home; he had not been away from Tadnol for twenty years. He spent the morning pleasantly in reading, to please himself, and in writing the lives of the kings of England, to please others.

He was a careful historian, and in his writing there was always quaintness and humour, each king being vested in more than his robes – having a fine halo sent down, direct from God to Mr Dottery's pen, to cover many royal infirmities.

But though Mr Dottery was an historian with an impartial mind – except in the matter of preference for kingly rule to any other form of government – yet he went so far as to say that Jack Cade – had he been trained differently – might have made a very good rural dean.

But, alas! Mr Dottery's quiet and his history had come to an end. He could not write now. He had heard that Saint Susanna had been seen, more than once, near to his study window, but that did not trouble him nor cause him to drink milk instead of cream. Canon Dibben was another matter to Saint Susanna.

Mr Dottery had noticed in *The Times* Canon Dibben's advancement from one point to another – a curate, a curate-in-charge, a vicar, a canon; so at the last, Miss Cockett, whom Dibben married, knew every piece of furniture in the drawing-room at the Bishop's palace at Portstown, and also how many times one had to ring the door-bell there before the door was opened.

Living so near to Mr Dottery – for Dodder Vicarage was but two short miles across the heath – a little of the peculiar behaviour of Mr Dibben and his wife came to the knowledge of those who lived at Tadnol.

Mrs Dibben had a fine nose for a sin. She would sniff about a village, as though she suspected a cat of misbehaviour. She would watch for ill-doings, like a vixen for the lame duck, and would send her husband out into the lanes to see what was done. She went out herself too, looking sharply at everyone, spying into their ways with the intent to lay a sin to their charge – 'a liar, he; that's a thieving old woman; young strumpet is Alice; and what's Mrs Joyner but a carrier of lewd tales?'

The more staid and sober any poor husband in Dodder might look, with a newspaper crammed into his waistcoat to keep out the cold, the more sin to him! 'A lecher, at the very least, or a drunkard!'

Where so many harmless ones are taken, how could Mr Dottery

escape? He was only two miles away, and Mrs Dibben had passed him once out walking.

'I am sure that he is immoral,' she said to her husband at tea-time. (Mr Dibben secretly took an extra slice of the Sunday cake, that had lived – though a little drily – till Tuesday.) 'He keeps a girl,' she said, 'for his pleasure.'

'Where?' asked Mr Dibben, with his mouth full.

'In the study cupboard,' replied his wife.

6 TOMMY TOOLE ASKS A QUESTION

AT Tadnol the river flows easily; it has no vice, and when it overflows, it floods so gently that only the cows notice the change.

The Tadnol people are like the river. If they move a little out of the way, only the children see them, and whoever goes a little too far into trouble always turns back before any hurt is done.

Those who live quietly are quick to notice any change. When Mr Dottery's name was mentioned in any conversation that went on at the house doors or by the green, a woman would say, when she parted from her gossip, ''Tisn't the same with him now as it used to be.'

But no one could say what really was the matter. Mrs Croot thought it might be the virgin of Tadnol, Saint Susanna, who did the mischief.

'They dead saints bain't to be trusted,' she said, 'for a dead saint may easily become a living sinner, and she be about more than ever, so folk do say.'

Mr Dottery had been wont to preach boldly, but now that he was under a cloud his sermons changed. He talked to himself rather than preached, speaking in so low a tone that no one could hear him, except the twin daughters of Farmer Spenke, who sat next to the pulpit.

Amongst other matters these girls heard him say, 'Honour not the malice of thine enemy too much, as to say thy misery comes from him. Dishonour not the complexion of the times so much, as to say thy misery comes from them.'

Mrs Spenke disagreed with Mrs Croot about the ghost; she did not think that Mr Dottery would pay any heed to a shadow. Mrs Spenke knew a better reason for his displeasure, she thought the cause was more simple.

Mrs Spenke met Mrs Truggin near the well, plucked her by the sleeve, and drew her aside. She had something to say that she did not wish anyone else to hear.

'Mrs Taste be a kind giver,' she began cunningly, 'who do carry good things about the village, yet it isn't to be believed that she can really make good Yorkshire pudding.'

Having fired her shot almost directly into Mrs Truggin's ear, she waited a few moments, and then said gently, ''Tis what might well trouble a reading man, for consider, the table be laid and all be ready, the knives be cleaned and the napkin in 's place, and here be come a fine sirloin, all roasted and brown, and the undercut ready to melt in thee's mouth – but the pudding ... '

'Alas!' cried Mrs Truggin.

'Heavy as lead,' responded Mrs Spenke.

Mrs Truggin groaned.

'If 'tain't the pudding 'tis they prayers,' she observed.

'And do Mr Dottery pray?' asked Mrs Spenke in astonishment.

'Yes, Lottie do hear 'e,' replied Mrs Truggin. 'And, what be worse, Lottie do fancy that God do answer 'e's prayer, for one still evening, when she were all alone in kitchen, knitting her jumper, she did hear someone whisper through keyhole.'

'But Mr Dottery don't pray in kitchen, do 'e?' asked Mrs Spenke anxiously.

'No, he never does that,' replied Mrs Truggin, 'but Lottie do think that God did answer at the wrong door.'

'Well, we all make mistakes sometimes,' said Mrs Spenke, and as she turned down the lane she said hurriedly, 'and all men do know that Satan do often hide between cheese and macaroni.'

John Toole, the landlord of the *Tadnol Arms*, had given no opinion as to what might be the matter with Mr Dottery. John Toole had two manners. He looked loftily about him when he walked out of doors, and looked stoopingly when indoors because of the low ceilings; but his son Tommy was not so proud.

Tommy left the young Spenke girls upon the river bridge to look at the trout after Mr Dottery's first sad sermon, and called at the Rectory to ask what had happened. He found Lottie there, and invited her to go with him for a few moments down a dark lane, for the question that he wished to ask of her was a private one.

Tommy led her on until he was sure that they were out of anyone's hearing, and then holding her firmly, and as near to himself as he could get her to go, he asked her – kissing her ear first to make sure that she heard him – 'Do 'ee think, Lottie Truggin, that Mr Dottery have a fancy for thee?'

Lottie sighed. ''E wouldn't have to ask I twice to be kind,' she answered, 'but, alas! there bain't no poor girl that 'e do want. No, Tommy Toole, if it bain't the colic, 'tis the Queen.'

7   AN EASY IMAGE

NOVEMBER is a slug, a black and slimy month; 'tis a heavy log fastened to the backside of the year that pulls into the mire the last summer days, making them weep miserably. November is an ugly ghoul. It strips the trees that hide the graveyard from sight, so that from the hill nearby each tombstone can be plainly seen. November tells tales of corruption; it terrifies the simple, and it made Mr Turtle and his wife decide to leave Madder.

Mr Turtle was a labourer, and strangely enough, he was afraid to die, and yet more afraid of being buried. At Madder the Turtles lived near the churchyard, and they wished to move.

The Turtles wished to move, but the Rector of Tadnol wished to stay where he was. He could not bring himself to go even a day's journey, though he had been ordered to. But Mr Dottery could do what a great many people can never do: he could dwell a long time upon a few words; he chewed and digested them as the minutes passed.

When Tommy Toole asked Lottie his question, Mr Dottery sat in his study with a book upon his knee.

The afternoon darkened. Mrs Taste brought in the lamp, and soon followed with the tea-tray. Mr Dottery ate and drank. Lottie carried the things away. Mr Dottery bent his head over his book. He placed the reading-lamp nearer, so that he could see the better. He brooded over the same words again, and kept them still under his eyes — 'Our senses should not, like petulant and wanton girls, wander into markets and theatres without just employment.'

'I have no wish,' mused Mr Dottery, 'to wander anywhere like a

31

petulant girl. Have my books deceived me? Have they shown me a world that is no world? Have I sat so long at them that my eyes can only see shadows outside my own mind? Has my view become distorted?

'Am I right in considering the human creatures that move and have their being so near to me as merely straws that the winds of time dance with for a tiny moment, and then lay them down when the music ceases, they being weary, but the winds never weary? Am I right to let all men and women pass with a gesture – a good-evening or a good-morning, as I go by – until they or I are laid along in the ground?

'Have I been too jealous over my time, and a too great hater of any sort of interruption? A poor man who comes to me to beg a pair of trousers is troublesome, his talk is about rabbits. A moth that wishes to die in my lamp dies before I stir.

'The afternoon sound of Truggin ringing the church bell when I have forgotten, and God forgive me, that the day was Sunday, has made me groan. Alas! I fear that I have in a manner become like unto one who is in hiding from God, and God, might not He – though I do not like to say so, and have no intention of doing so – wish me to go out like a wanton girl, ring the Bishop's private door-bell at Portstown, and ask for admission?

'Are all wanton girls,' considered Mr Dottery, 'petulant too? Is it proper that I, who have lived so long, should know so little about young women – less, indeed, than I know about gobies and starfish? Should I not, sometime or other – in order to enlarge my experience of God's strange doings – have talked with one of them? All that I have done so far – I say it now to my shame – is to give presents to my niece, Barbara, who never even remembers to thank me for them.

'But, alas! girls are not books. Had Mrs Dibben been a folio of Dryden I might have spoken to her on the day when I met her on the heath out walking. But she had no decent cover like my large volume of *Hall's Commentaries*, and, if a young woman's heart were opened, I fear that one would find other matter there than hexameter lines.'

Mr Dottery closed the book gently, but murmured almost fiercely, 'I will go no further ... '

During this Sunday evening, while Mr Dottery was thinking that many a young woman would be much better bound in a plain cover, those who sat at the Tadnol inn took their beer but sadly.

Outside the inn, the sign of which, painted upon a board, was a great fish that looked like a sea-serpent, except that it had the tail of a bream, there was no comfort. A steady rain had begun to fall, and Landlord Toole, seeing the melancholy looks of those within, peeped out of the door to see only weeping clouds there. They told him – as those funereal clouds often will – that soon Truggin, or a fellow-tradesman, would bury each one of them.

Mr Toole returned to the parlour in time to see Truggin kill out of pity the last summer fly, that, a moment before, had become entangled in a spider's web. Mr Truggin took up the fly by its wing and, digging a little hole in the sawdust of the spittoon, he buried the fly – and looked happier.

Blacksmith Croot leaned heavily over the table, and, in a little puddle of spilt beer, discerned another blacksmith, exactly like himself, who seemed to be – for the reflected flames and the inn fire flickered and danced – beating a ponderous piece of iron, that gave out sparks that rose up into his own brain and told him that he must one day die.

For some minutes the sober ticking of Mr Toole's clock was the only sound to be heard, and then Truggin observed mournfully:

'Mr Dottery don't eat nor drink as he used. Only yesterday a great fish, as large as what be painted on signboard, were brought in to 'is dinner, and that great fish went out same as 'e did come in.'

Farmer Spenke raised his mug to his lips in gloomy silence, but he put the cup down without tasting the beer. He drew a long breath, and his mouth opened widely.

'What be we?' he exclaimed. 'Only blamed fools to let a poor man, who be kind to all, live so sad? Who be there amongst us who have been bold enough to ask him what be the matter, and what it be that do so torment and hurt him?'

'We will go,' cried Landlord Toole, starting up, and for the first time in his life he hit his head against the ceiling, 'and ask of Mr Dottery where the flea do tickle ... '

The hour was ten, and Lottie Truggin, after helping Mrs Taste to wash and dry the dinner-plates from the dining-room and the supper-plates from their own table, sat herself down, exactly in front of the kitchen fire, with her knitting in her lap. Mrs Taste took her usual chair and held a Bible in her hands. Lottie looked at the Bible and smiled.

'I was only thinking just now,' she said, beginning to knit, 'about Samuel, for when I was confirmed the second time, at Shelton – I liked the walk there – the sermon was about him.'

'Be careful you don't drop a stitch,' said Mrs Taste, 'for I can't be always picking them up for you.'

'I do wonder,' observed Lottie, 'if God do ever speak to girls.'

'Oh no,' said Mrs Taste, 'I am sure He never does, at least not in the way that you mean, though' – and Mrs Taste blushed – 'there was, of course – '

Lottie started. Sounds were heard, heavy steps in the Rectory drive. ''Tis men,' she cried.

'The bell-ringers,' said Mrs Taste, who had grown a little drowsy.

'No,' returned Lottie, fearfully, ''tain't Christmas yet.'

A knock came at the back door.

'I will go,' said Mrs Taste, 'instead of you, Lottie, and see who it is.'

When she had seated her visitors, like a half-hoop round the kitchen fire – Lottie having removed herself, a little grudgingly, to let the men come nearer – Mrs Taste went to the study door.

But she did not knock. Mr Dottery was reading aloud to himself, and she would not disturb him. She decided to return to the kitchen for a little and come again.

Mr Dottery still read on aloud – he did so sometimes, as a compliment to good writing – 'Whom men could not honour in presence' – Mr Dottery's voice sounded very lonely – 'because they dwelt far off, they took the counterfeit of his image from far, and made an express image of a king whom they honoured, to the end that by this their forwardness they might flatter him that was absent, as if he were present.'

Mr Dottery groaned.

'Alas!' he pondered, 'I am no sculptor, and I fear that I could make but a sorry image of Bishop Ashbourne out of Tadnol clay.'

Mr Dottery's mind ventured to see the matter in another way.

'Would it,' he wondered, 'be a sin to wish that God had allowed man's image – the counterfeit of man – to be seen in the earth, instead of man himself? In my own short walks I have noticed that many a rugged tree-trunk has a striking resemblance to a man, and many a great rough clod – if one regards it long enough – takes the human form – and many a cloud might well be an old woman in the sky.

'Trees and clods and cloud-shapes pass on their way, dissolve or change, when their short moments, or little years, are ended. They do not fear angry letters, they dread no journeys. Might not men – though 'tis not for the pot to direct the potter's hand – have been made of some light stuff, so that they might move, free as the night winds, delighting to bathe in the harmless showers of God's love, moving easily and always happily.

'Surely,' thought Mr Dottery, 'all those large purposes for which, wise men say, the Creator made man, might be easily perfected and completed if soap-bubbles had been supplied instead of fleshly bodies. As a boy, I used to blow bubbles, and if God had made men and women of this milky froth, they would have moved with the wind and have been able to obey their spiritual master, the Bishop, with a ready obedience.

'And could not I – if things were as simple as that – make an image too? If men were but weeds, if the Bishop were a pink and Mr Dibben a hollyhock, would they ever have troubled their heads if only one girl came as a candidate for confirmation?'

Mrs Taste softly knocked at the door.

MR DOTTERY'S company broke in upon him as he sat in his chair in deep dejection. The *Apocrypha* lay near to him, open upon the table.

'I have been considering,' said Mr Dottery, after Truggin – as became one who belonged to the family – had found chairs for the guests, 'that although it is a true and a wise saying that "to obey is better than sacrifice, and to hearken than the fat of rams," yet obedience, alas! when one is used, and ever has been, to pleasing oneself in every little way, is often almost impossible to a poor sinner.

'I see now,' said Mr Dottery, speaking to himself as much as to the company, 'that a man who prides himself in preaching obedience to others, and telling them, as I have often done, that when any master or spiritual pastor calls even from far, to come, they should at once obey him, should be obedient too. But alas! 'tis easier to tell another to climb Mount Everest than to do it oneself, for I find it impossible to obey.'

'No, no,' said Truggin, edging near to his master, so as to show him the greater sympathy, '"tain't impossible to obey Death; nor be it hard to get buried, if fee be paid.'

Mr Dottery smiled. He knew the contentment and pleasure that Truggin had in his art. He sat silent and looked upon his friends, as though he wondered for the first time why they had come.

Landlord Toole had once been a horse-doctor. He regarded Mr Dottery as he had once regarded an old stallion belonging to Farmer Lord of Shelton, which had hurt its back.

'Thee bain't well,' he said, 'and we be come to drench 'ee – to make 'ee better.'

'My good neighbour,' replied Mr Dottery, speaking tenderly – for he was touched by the coming of his friends – 'I am well enough and require no medicine.'

'There be something the matter wi' 'ee,' urged Farmer Spenke, 'and that we be sure of. Maybe 'tis something that thee do want, that thee don't like to tell we of, for a learned gentleman may want some things, I believe, as well as a poor man.'

Blacksmith Croot struck his knee with his fist: the dust flew up.

'Spenke,' he cried, 'thee do know something. There be wants that do come to all; who be there who do pass a signboard without wishing to enter and taste?'

'And who,' cried Truggin, overcome by the excitement of the moment, 'do pass a green churchyard without wishing that 'e were laid in a grave?'

Farmer Spenke rose and beckoned, and Toole, Card, Croot, and Truggin retired with him into a corner of the study, where they commenced to talk together in whispers, as a jury might who had to decide upon a verdict in the presence of the prisoner.

Mr Dottery remained in his chair; he even lay back a little more reposefully and closed his eyes.

Men who whisper at first, will, when the plot thickens and the subject waxes warmer, soon talk louder, and it was not long before Mr Dottery heard something of what was said.

Farmer Spenke was speaking. ''Twas my brother's,' said the farmer angrily, as though one of the company had cast a doubt upon his words, 'and because thik poor bull weren't allowed to get to they young heifers, 'e went so sad that 'e did only mope in pasture.'

'I do know thee's rich brother wi' all his lands wouldn't starve a creature,' observed John Card, in a soothing tone.

'No, no,' replied Farmer Spenke, 'me fine brother weren't like that. All the cake, corn, roots, grass, old hay that a poor beast mid want to make 'im lively were 'is to devour, and yet 'e did pine and languish.'

''Tis strange indeed,' muttered Croot.

'And the field where thik bull did bide were called the Parlour,' said Spenke; 'and, what be queerer still, the little warm paddock nearby, that did belong to me brother's neighbour, were named the Kitchen.'

'Were there any stock kept in thik kitchen?' asked John Card.

'The young heifers,' replied the farmer; 'but nothing could be done – so me brother did say – for thik poor bull.'

'Thee's brother never thought of showing him a grave,' remarked Truggin, 'for a wise bull mid prefer that to a wedding- dance wi' a young cow.'

The men spoke lower. But presently, Landlord Toole said in a loud whisper to Farmer Spenke, ''E do lack a maiden.'

The word awoke the mind of John Card.

'Though I be only a poor man and no clergyman,' he said loudly, 'yet I do know how 'tis wi' me own self, for when I be a-sweeping of a chimney, setting one rod into another to reach the further, I do often mind that a chimney bain't a woman.'

'They be womanish,' said Blacksmith Croot with a sigh, 'when they do smoke.'

Mr Dottery had taken up a book, and was reading again.

Farmer Spenke was a faithful churchman, he knew religion. When he was drunk, he remembered God, and when he was sober he would think of Mr Dottery. He now called to mind one of Mr Dottery's sermons, that he had listened to more wakefully than usual.

He remembered that Mr Dottery had observed that someone – some great lord – had given his well-beloved Son to save mankind. That was indeed a kind act, and Farmer Spenke thought that he might perform another. He had no son to give away, but he had two daughters – twins. Why should he not copy God's goodness, nay, enlarge upon it, and present both his daughters to Mr Dottery?

When five men all nod to one another at the same moment, 'tis a sign they are agreed.

Farmer Spenke stepped forward, and Mr Dottery, seeing that the discussion was ended, closed his book too.

'We have found out thee's pain,' said Farmer Spenke in a loud voice, searching Mr Dottery with his eyes, 'and we do know where 'tis.'

'We'll bring thee a medicine,' said Truggin.

Blacksmith Croot pressed forward.

''Tain't well to hammer too quickly,' he cried, pushing Truggin aside, 'or nail mid cut into soft hoof and horse go lame. 'Tis best to raise 'is leg slow, or 'e mid kick. Leave 'e to I to doctor. Farmer Spenke don't mean to frighten 'ee,' he said, smiling; ''e don't mean no doctor's knife, thee bain't in need of nothing like that, we do know. 'E be only telling 'ee of a filly or two who bain't kickers.'

''E do mean they twin sisters,' said Toole.

Farmer Spenke was aware that two drinks are better than one, if the cordial be of the right kind, and he said generously, holding out both his hands as if he held a daughter in each of them, 'Have the both of them, do 'ee breed as fast as thee can, for 'tis said in country places that love children be the best milkers.'

Truggin came forward. He was not going to be outdone by the farmer's kindness.

'Me granddaughter, Lottie,' he whispered to Mr Dottery, 'who do bide in thee's own kitchen – and no Lent don't see she a-fasting – be plump and saucy, and be worth looking at wi' only she's chemise to cover up all her prettiness. I bain't one to hold back when others be kind, and maybe they Spenke maids bain't doers of the word but only talkers, but our Lottie do always say she do fancy a man rather than they finicking boys.'

Truggin paused for breath.

'Take all of them, sir,' said John Card, who knew what he himself would have wished for.

For the second time that evening Mr Dottery smiled.

'I am extremely obliged to you, my friends,' he said, 'for the offer that you have so generously made to me of your three handmaidens. But don't you think that if Canon Dibben knew that I intended to ease my melancholy in the way that you suggest and wish to make so easy, that might, you suppose, give me the happiness of Adam or of Jove, he would think ill of me?'

'But we wouldn't,' laughed Truggin, 'for to diddle-daddle a maid be the next best thing to burying her.'

'But it would be,' said Mr Dottery, 'a romantic story for Mr Dibben to tell the Bishop. And now, will you be so kind as to ring the bell, Truggin?'

Mrs Taste was soon in attendance.

'I have invited you to come to me, Mrs Taste, so that I may tell you, and these kind neighbours, what is really the trouble. Ever since the Confirmation was held here, I have received letters, one every week – and sometimes two.'

'I knew it was a letter,' exclaimed Mrs Taste.

'Many letters, Mrs Taste,' said Mr Dottery, 'and none of them kind. But I did not think that anyone here would notice my dejection, though, do what I could, it was impossible for me to appear as con- tented as of old.

'You are all good people, and are kind to one another, with a true kindness – a kindness that, I fear, is not universal. Soon after that unlucky Confirmation – though not unlucky for Lottie, I trust – Canon Dibben began to tell tales to the Bishop. He told him I permit the people here to do what they choose, to be a law to themselves, that they are all of them loose-livers, wine- drinkers — '

''Tis a lie,' cried Toole.

'And that I only hold one service a week, and that the one candidate who was confirmed here had been already confirmed elsewhere two or three times.'

Truggin nodded. 'And didn't I tell she,' he remarked to Mr Croot, 'that it weren't true religion to make a dance frock out of they white veils that Mr Dottery do give free?'

'A letter came to me,' said Mr Dottery, very mournfully, 'this very morning, telling me that unless I presented myself at the Palace at Portstown to reply to these charges, proceedings would be taken against me in the ecclesiastical court. I should be inhibited from preaching and, no doubt, turned out of Tadnol – and I shall never find another cellar so cool for College wine. The last letter was not, I think, written by the Bishop himself, but by his lady, who is a friend of Mrs Dibben's, and whose maiden name was Pettifer.'

''Tain't a good name for a maiden,' observed Landlord Toole.

'No, no,' said Spenke, 'and 'tain't no wonder that she wished to change it, though to marry a holy bishop be a strange thing to do.'

'No, no, farmer,' said Truggin, 'nothing in they holy ways be strange to a lady, who do know a bishop's doings same as we do know — '

Mr Dottery's clock struck twelve.

'At first I hoped,' said Mr Dottery wearily, 'when I received the letter this morning that I should be courageous enough to go when next Friday comes – for that is the last day of grace given to me – to reply to these charges. But I know now that I cannot even bring my thoughts to contemplate this visit to Portstown, which would mean perhaps that I might have to take luncheon at the Palace.'

Mrs Taste held up her hands in horror.

'The saucepans,' she cried 'I am sure that none are properly scoured, for in a religious house like the Bishop's, the cook must be always praying, and the kitchenmaid would never disturb her to say that the potatoes were burnt.'

Mrs Taste opened the door, and Mr Dottery's visitors departed. They went off thoughtfully, as though they wondered what could be done to heal so sad a sore.

Mr Dottery turned to his books. He put the *Apocrypha* aside and took up Lucretius, a passage of which he translated into the vulgar tongue.

"Thy life being once gone, nothing shall live after thee."

'How then can it be possible,' considered Mr Dottery, 'that Ashbourne, with whom I used to read when we were at Benet's – while this Dibben was yet in the straw – how can it be possible, when all things die with us when we die – every candle going out like our candle – to hurt and torment one another as we do, when we are, as we all must be, in present view of utter destruction? And these poor Tadnol people, how can they be harmed by sitting in the autumn sunshine rather than by crouching in a pew, with their knees touching their chins?

'Doth not God Himself – so near goeth the countryman to His doings – chirp as a sparrow on a plough, or lie as an autumn leaf driven into quietude at the bottom of an empty wagon? Surely a man whose years are over fifty – a man who is settled quietly and is content with his life – should be exempted from the scolding of a master for a petty fault, from the tale-telling of a Dibben, from the inquisitive malice of idle women.

'In this corner where I live,' sighed Mr Dottery, 'I have tried to be kind.'

9   MR DOTTERY SAYS 'NO'

SOMETIMES, the month of November being come – when the almanac gives a picture of a man driving a wedge into a fallen tree, while the rain falls down – Nature, that monstrous and sudden lover, embraces anew the earth with a loving kiss of summer sunshine. The air is clear then, for the October rains have made it so, and the long afternoon shadows, thrown by the great Tadnol elms, please a peaceful mind, while the warm sun – a pretty last blessed gift from an already forgotten summer – gladdens the hearts of those who are wise enough to live in the present moment.

The morning after Mr Dottery had been visited by his neighbours who had hoped to do him a service, he was sitting, as was his custom, in the Tadnol Rectory study.

Of one thing Mr Dottery had always been sure – that all fuss and clamour, all hurry and excitement, are unbecoming to a churchman. Feeling so, he had ever allowed the Spirit of God to work – and who dares say that it does not? – in the hearts of the people of Tadnol, believing that God in His mercy would save them all, as well as the blind moles and the little red squirrels, in His own good time.

But now Mr Dottery's thoughts were difficult to him. He could not free himself from his own bonds. He was no casuist; it was no use his trying to explain away the fact that the Bishop of Portstown was in authority over him. Mr Dottery had always insisted upon – in his writings and elsewhere – a strict obedience to the church and to the king. And now that a proper command had come to him, he felt that he ought to obey.

Mr Dottery rose from his chair, he stood with his back to the fire, and looked down at the study floor.

He had already – for he had left the breakfast-table half an hour before – taken from the drawer his work for the morning. A sunbeam found its way into his room, giving a golden hue to the plain brown cover of the *Letters of Erasmus*, written in Latin to King Henry VIII. Mr Dottery was surprised. He regarded earnestly this yellow beam of light streaming into his room, as though he expected to read therein – written in Greek and in Latin – a reprieve.

But no reprieve was written there, and Mr Dottery groaned. He began to look at his room as though he might soon have to leave it. He looked lovingly, for it was his corner in which he did as he wished. He regarded his room as an old red fox might have smelt at a well-worn earth for the last time, knowing that in a day or two the hunters would come with a nasty little dog and dig him out of it.

He had, alas! often read an Elizabethan homily instead of preaching a sermon. He might, he believed, be turned out for that alone, so sadly is the church changed in these latter days.

Mr Dottery looked at the bookcase again: the beams of light had left Erasmus to shine upon the *Holy Bible*. Mr Dottery took the book into his hands and opened it at random, hoping to find counsel there.

"That I may not seem," he read, "as if I would terrify you by letters."

'But you have terrified me,' groaned Mr Dottery. 'But what is this?' and he read a little further – "And so you need not go to the regions beyond."

'Indeed,' Mr Dottery reflected, 'I cannot go. If I did go' – and Mr Dottery shivered uneasily – 'I should be obliged to rise at seven, descend the stairs before the house is properly warmed, eat a woeful breakfast with my eyes fixed upon the clock, and have no time to open the paper to learn the health of the king. I should then have to leave my Bible, leave my study chair that I am accustomed to write in, leave my warm rug that I gather round my knee as I write, leave my fireside. Indeed, I cannot go.'

And then the Reverend Silas Dottery, being a patrician and free-born, began to wonder: 'Was this final command that he had received a proper one? Should a bishop of the Elizabethan Church – to quote a cardinal – have a wife at all? A great English queen, the first Protestant, thought not. What right or title, then, had a plain Mrs Ashbourne to order a scholar to leave his books – a scholar who now and again suffered from the commands of the gout, that queen of diseases – and upon a fool's errand, too.'

What reason could be given that Lottie Truggin should not be confirmed once, twice, or a dozen times? She was but making her soul's salvation the surer for it.

And so Mr Dottery reasoned, but all the time he knew that he did wrong in not obeying the command.

'And after all,' he considered, 'it is a simple thing to do – a short journey.' But the mornings were beginning to be dark and, if he rose at seven, he would have to dress by candlelight – 'a troublesome beginning,' he thought.

Mr Dottery kept in his bedroom a manuscript copy, in his own handwriting, of *Areopagitica* – that he had himself done into Greek – and he would always read a few lines of this book before venturing to come down to breakfast.

And now he thought, 'Could he read *Areopagitica* with one wax candle?'

Mr Dottery shook his head, and never had such a gesture said more finally, 'I cannot go.'

'But will no one,' he wondered, seeing a last chance in this hope, 'go in my place to argue with this great Ashbourne? Oh, would that Saint Susanna were here!'

He heard a soft knock at the door.

'Come in,' said Mr Dottery, believing that the virgin saint who appeared sometimes in Tadnol, when least expected, would enter his room.

'Come in,' said Mr Dottery, the second time.

Lottie Truggin stood before him.

10 A MESSAGE FROM GOD

LOTTIE TRUGGIN, the granddaughter of the sexton, had been born in Tadnol, christened in Tadnol, and confirmed once in Tadnol. During all Lottie's sixteen years, in which she had peeped, run, laughed and worked, nothing had, so far, disturbed her heart, unless it were a certain friendliness that she had for Mr Dottery's surplice.

The wish to have a nearer acquaintance than the Rectory pew gave to her with that surplice was always with her, and when she was but twelve she would skip lightly from her parents' house – throwing a merry word at Tommy Toole, who followed her – up to her grandmother Truggin's door, and beg to be allowed to iron the surplice.

While she did so Lottie, bending over her work, would say determinedly: 'Tain't no village boy that I do want, 'tis a clergyman.'

'Oh, do thee be careful,' Mrs Truggin would reply, 'don't 'ee burn 'en now thee be got to middle ... '

Even though Lottie had entered so bravely into Mr Dottery's study, now that she was there she felt frightened. In order to succeed in her mission it was necessary that Mr Dottery should be a greater silly than she had ever expected him to be. It was one thing to take a command from her grandfather and to get into her cunning little head what she had to say, but it was quite another matter to go right into Mr Dottery's room and to tell the story.

In order to give herself courage Lottie looked at the bookcase.

'If he reads all those dry old books,' she decided, 'then he must be simple ... I be come with a message,' she said boldly.

'From whom?' inquired Mr Dottery, without raising his head.

'From God Almighty,' said Lottie.

Mr Dottery looked at God's messenger, who neither winced, nor stirred, nor showed any fear.

Mr Dottery expressed no fear either. He was no Eli: he had no sons. Neither was he unbelieving, for as one who loved good books and holy ways, he had ever been the bridegroom of divinity, and so, ready for a call.

To some, every old story is but a fancy, an unreal fable, and as good as blotted out by time. To Mr Dottery Scripture was truth, and the same God, who is the first as well as the last, and who had called 'Samuel, Samuel,' might, if He saw the need for it, call 'Lottie' too.

Lottie was right; Mr Dottery was a simple kind of man. In a great many ways he was exactly like a child. Indeed, a deep reader, who has meditated much in solitude and without hardship, has often that very quality of childlikeness that is alluded to in the Gospels. And Mr Dottery was never one to suspect a jest.

When the door had opened he had really expected that Saint Susanna might have come in. He had always held that virginity was a thing becoming to a dead saint. He had read the story of Daphnis and Chloe, and the marriage of Cupid and Psyche, as well as the Holy Gospels. Some virgins, he knew, were hard put to it. One had borne a Son, the Saviour of the world; others had been less fortunate.

In Tadnol, since the days of Saint Susanna, who saw visions, and as likely as not received messages from God, there had, Mr Dottery knew, been other virgins as chaste and as pious as she. And if others had heard God speak, why should not Lottie Truggin?

'What is the thing,' asked Mr Dottery, 'that the Lord hath said unto thee? Does He bid me take a joyful journey to Himself, or is it His will that I should go to Portstown?'

'No,' replied Lottie, 'He has bid me go to see Bishop Ashbourne instead of you.'

'Do not hide anything from me of all the things that He said unto thee,' urged Mr Dottery.

'He told me,' answered Lottie, 'that I was to go straight to the Bishop's Palace and ring the front-door bell. He said that I mustn't stay in the street to look at the shops, and that I mustn't smile at the fellows, but keep on the pavement for fear of being run over.'

'Anything else?' asked Mr Dottery.

'Yes, He told me the times of the trains, and how long it takes to walk from the Palace to the station.'

Mr Dottery drew a deep breath.

'I thank Him,' he said.

Lottie turned to go.

'Have you remembered to ask Mrs Taste for a holiday on Friday?' he inquired.

'No,' answered Lottie.

'Then give Mrs Taste my compliments,' said Mr Dottery, 'and tell her that I allow you to go.'

And Mr Dottery, who could not do less for Lottie now that she was God's messenger, rose and opened the door for her.

Returning to his place before the fire, Mr Dottery saw that the beam of light was still in the room. It had moved from Erasmus to the Bible, and now it shone upon the dull brown of the *Original Letters* relative to the English Reformation.

TADNOL is a village where the heath is the hill. And although the heath is but a little above the village, yet to those who lived at Tadnol it often seemed to be in the clouds.

Tadnol possessed one street, beside which – though a little retired – were the church and Rectory. There was also a lane or two, and there was the river. Most of the cottages in Tadnol stood on either side of the street, with the exception of the inn, which was a short distance down one of the lanes. By the side of each cottage along the street there was a tall elm tree. The river, though hidden by trees, is but a little way off the main village, and each path that does not go to the heath goes to the river.

The Tadnol river is sacred to Saint Susanna. Her ghost has been seen sometimes upon its banks and even in the water. At other times Susanna has been seen on the green, or running away from the Rectory.

Everyone in the neighbourhood believed in Saint Susanna, except Mrs Dibben, the wife of the Vicar of Dodder – though she thought that there was a strange girl who existed in Tadnol, who wasn't a saint.

But in Tadnol the story of Saint Susanna will always be remembered and believed, though the exact date when she lived is unknown. Saint Susanna was only seventeen years old when she died. She was praying upon the green. Her bare legs attracted the wanton eyes of a ravisher, she fled to the river and was drowned, praying.

Mr Dottery always wondered how such an evil deed as this could find a home in Tadnol history. He could only suppose that the Holy Spirit was not the only one who sows seeds in the lanes, and that there is another sower of a different kind, whose evil seeds were not always picked up by little children for their pea-shooters, and some of them might very well be found and devoured by the unwary. Susanna's ravisher must have eaten this devil's food.

The sunbeams that had brought the remembrance of Saint Susanna to Mr Dottery had, while he was thinking of her, moved further, past the *Poetical Works of William Wordsworth* to illuminate *Gotthold's Emblems*.

While the sun waited there, Mr Dottery felt a curious wish – for his sadness was lifted – to walk beside the river and to see Susanna. Once before she had been seen on the fifth day of November.

The hour was about twelve when Mr Dottery walked out. And now a strange thing happened that could only occur to a scholar, in a village that had a saint.

Mr Dottery had not reached his own drive gate before a new and unlooked-for thought came to him. Had he been always right to think only of himself and of his studies and to neglect all other human matters?

What had Tadnol been to him? Only another Cambridge College – another Benet's. The fields and the lanes were the cloisters and shady walks. The pigs in the paths and a goat or two that he met had been to him but other Fellows of the same college, and an old bull of Farmer Spenke's, that he met one day, he mistook for the Dean. Even the Tadnol weather had only made him turn the more eagerly to his books.

In the spring, when the sun shone and the flowers began to show themselves in the Rectory garden, Mr Dottery would peruse Anacreon and turn an ode into English verse, as a compliment to the first rosebud. Upon sad days, when the winter winds outside his windows troubled the bare trees, he would stand at his study window, with a finger in Euripides, and look towards the heath, above which the frightened crows were circling. If the March wind blew cold, he would read some choice fragments from the familiar discourse of that godly, learned man and famous champion of God's Truth – Dr Martin Luther.

Mr Dottery had made his study a home for his mind and body. There he meant to live and die without interruption, reading in the original until his eyes should fail him, and hoping that, if that trial came to him, he would be permitted to close them for ever.

His books were his pleasure; all other pleasures in the world he mistrusted, though he permitted to himself old wine as a good seasoning to the old tongues.

Coming into the country and seeing himself immured there, he began to learn husbandry from Virgil, and invited Truggin to interpret to him the cries of Tadnol, so that he might not – being a bachelor – mistake the screams of a ringled pig for the outcries of a newborn infant.

'Living as I do in the country,' he had told Archdeacon Ford in a letter, some time before our story commences, 'one is a little more subject to temptation than when one resides in college. I mean that there's always the danger of letting one's breakfast-time slide imperceptibly into the luncheon hour. One is also tempted to linger at night over a bottle, when what we ought to do is to say our prayer and go to bed. But God pardon me if I am become a sluggard!'

Mr Dottery had lived a long time in the country before any improper incursion into his realm happened. Though once, when after

54

breakfast he had settled himself upon his study chair and opened the book that he was reading, he had been disturbed by a great shouting and hallooing of men, the noise of dogs, and the galloping of horses outside in the lane.

'An invasion of the Parthians,' murmured Mr Dottery. He went to the window, and opened it widely to see what was going forward, without waiting to think whether a spear or an arrow would transfix him.

In the garden he saw a hare that ran lightly across the lawn and leaped, without the least hesitation, into the open window of the study with the hounds close behind her. Mr Dottery closed the window with a bang. He did so, wishing to show kindness to the poor creature that was being run after by the hounds, who had nearly had their fangs in her soft fur. When he shut the window Mr Dottery turned to his chair as though to read again. But instead, he looked at the hare.

Now that she was there with him he began to feel a little perturbed, not knowing how the hare would behave herself. He had often been alone with God, but he had not, until that morning, been alone with a hare.

Mr Dottery stood near to the window. The hare crouched near to the bookcase. They looked at one another. The creature appeared to be more surprised than frightened, and, as Mr Dottery regarded her attentively, noting her long lean body and her wild strange eyes, hc began to feel the more uneasy of the two, and wished, like the frog in the fable, to take himself out of her way.

He was uncertain of hcr behaviour, and did not know what he ought to do to tame her and keep her quiet. He wondered if it would content and please the hare if he were to read to her, in Latin, the story of Androcles and the Lion.

The more doubtful Mr Dottery was of what he ought to do to please his guest, the more skittish became the hare. She leapt upon the table, upsetting the inkpot over the book that Mr Dottery had left open. After doing that she commenced an act even more devastating to the feelings of a peaceful man: she sprang amongst Mr Dottery's most precious books and began to dig with her sharp claws.

Mr Dottery looked at her in consternation. Was she a witch? Had she come there to tear his books to pieces and then to attack him? Ought he to defend himself?

Mr Dottery was considering what weapon to arm himself with, when the Master of the Hunt – Lord Bullman – with the prerogative of a peer, burst into the room and, after an exciting chase that lasted for ten minutes, during which everything was overturned, at last caught his prey. A few moments later, when Mr Dottery had called Mrs Taste to see the mischief that was done, the good man prayed aloud – 'From lightning and tempest, from the beasts of the field and from all huntsmen, from murder and from sudden death, Good Lord deliver us.'

Mrs Taste said 'Amen.'

Mr Dottery opened his drive gate. He had never, as far as he could recollect, opened that gate before to walk out in the morning. He hoped he was not becoming a wanton. He strode down the lane that led to the river.

It was proper, as he felt so strangely himself that morning, that he should think about miracles.

A miracle he knew to be any marvel that occurs. If a cat gives a mouse its freedom, if an upper servant forgets the pride of her place, if a lawyer forgives a debt, a miracle has happened.

'But to perceive a miracle,' Mr Dottery reflected, 'one's state of mind must be holy. One must be clean, one must have forgiven all one's enemies.' Mr Dottery hoped he was in a fit state to see Saint Susanna.

No one knew less about the domestic economy of his own house than did Mr Dottery. He left all things to Mrs Taste. He was not aware that Lottie Truggin had asked for an hour or two to run and tell her grandfather the success of the plan that the inspired drinkers had evoked at the inn to end Mr Dottery's trouble.

Except on her way to church, when he never looked at her, Mr Dottery had not seen Lottie out of doors, when a girl is quite another thing to a servant. And how was he to know that, after telling Truggin the news while he ate his dinner, and having a little time to spare, Lottie had run down to the river to paddle.

Mr Dottery had never been one to blame the Reformation for every trouble that happened in the world. He was of it, in all its ways that were good. But he had always preached that righteous zeal could be carried too far. To pray to the saints was one thing – for to God alone we ought to pray – but to believe in the saints was another matter.

Mr Dottery had always shown a lively interest in the ghost of Saint Susanna. That Susanna, in her lifetime, should have been bold enough to pray in public – upon the village green – pleased him.

He knew that in country places the gross fellows would be likely to take a maid at a disadvantage if they caught her upon her knees, with her head in her hands. Truggin had told him much, and Truggin knew Tadnol.

Mr Dottery liked to think of Susanna. Sometimes, in his bed, he would think of her, before he went to sleep. The idea of this holy virgin who had once lived in Tadnol – the daughter of a poor turf-cutter, so it was said – had always delighted him. That most women in the country, as well as elsewhere, led the lives of sparrows, as Truggin always said, did not take away, but gave the greater glory, to the few virgins that remained chaste.

There was another reason, besides her goodness, that made Mr Dottery wish to meet Saint Susanna. He believed that she was the only person, dead or alive, in Tadnol, who understood Latin. When Susanna prayed upon the green she must have prayed in Latin, and no saint would pray in a tongue that she did not understand. Mr Dottery was most eager to see her.

Mr Dottery walked along by the river path. The November sun, with a wholesome softness, warmed the air. Late, coloured flowers upon the banks of the river still bloomed. Mr Dottery stood for a moment and looked at the cool flowing waters of the river. The beauty that he saw made him sad. A splendid green dragonfly hovered over the water weeds, while, in the meadow nearby, Farmer Spenke's cows were lying fast asleep.

The river path turned suddenly, and Mr Dottery turned with it, coming to a place where the waters spread out like a lake. Upon the bank two girls were resting. These girls were Nellie and Betty, the twin daughters of Farmer Spenke, of whom it was said that only Tommy Toole knew the difference – and that only when he was alone with one of them. The girls were looking at something in the water, and Mr Dottery looked too – he saw Saint Susanna.

SAINT SUSANNA

She was in the middle of the river; her legs were bare, and she was trying to catch a minnow. She showed more of herself even than she had done kneeling upon the green to pray, when the then parish priest – for, alas! the truth must out – had cast her down to do his wicked will, and when she struggled and escaped had followed her to the river and, some say, drowned her there.

Mr Dottery gazed at Saint Susanna with admiration. She was not praying now, she was catching minnows. But in either appearance she was equally attractive. She must have come from heaven at that very moment to play with the little fish in the river that once drowned her. And at any moment she would return to the skies.

Saint Susanna turned and saw him, and hid her face in her petticoat – her frock was already tucked up.

Mr Dottery could not avoid looking at her, for the ghost of a saint is not often to be seen. And as he looked, he forgave – as he hoped to be forgiven – the Reverend John Ambrose, the priest of Tadnol in the year of Our Lord thirteen hundred and thirty-three.

THOUGH a miracle had perhaps happened in Tadnol, and Mr Dottery had seen Saint Susanna almost as near and as living as ever did that poor drunken John Ambrose, whose one moment's folly damned him for ever, yet in the gay city of Portstown God played none of his pranks, but permitted all things to go on according to the laws that He ordained when He made the world.

In March at Portstown the fleas were as merry as March fleas always are, setting a copy for the sinners of the town who but tamely followed in their wake, for who can be as merry as a flea? Feeling discouraged in their exercises – that brought some of the young women to tears – the sinners reformed and attended the cathedral to hear the Bishop preach, and there was no miracle in that.

There had been nothing miraculous either about the marriage of Miss Agnes Pettifer to Bishop Ashbourne, who had been raised up, by God's hand, into higher authority. Indeed, all that had happened in the matter of this marriage would hardly have excited the curiosity of a spider, who would of course be aware that every woman likes a large web.

Often a marriage that is not directly arranged by Providence is brought about by some chance event that might happen to anyone. A change of clothes is, as every churchman knows, a necessary part of a rise in place, and a bishop, though he still retains some of the garments that he wore as a plain clergyman, yet is obliged by custom – that commenced in a penance – to wear an apron.

It has been writ as a gloss in the ancient fable of the Wolf in Sheep's

Clothing that the beast, when he first covered his own mangy pelt with a fair sheepskin, found himself a little hindered and troubled by the weight of it. He could not now, as he had been used to do in his old merry way, lop and loll along in the forest, nor yet roll to ease the itch of his back in the dust or snow. He could not, either, at the first putting on of his new coat, discover his mate, for the sheepskin hung over his eyes as near to blind him, and, although he barked as loudly as he could, telling his bitch that 'twas only a trick to catch a ewe-lamb, she nevertheless trotted off to find another husband.

The poor wolf began to wish all such changes of raiment to the devil, for though the purpose of the change – as it often is in other walks of life – was for the good and comfort of his belly, yet its wear was tedious. And besides, when he considered the matter a little further, this covering himself with such a pitiful cheating contrivance was extremely distasteful to his sense of honour as a bold wolf, who could as well leap into a fold and get a sheep as another.

Remaining for a while under a lonely pine tree that was as high as a cathedral steeple, rather sad and pensive, the wolf was reproached by his comrades for his faint-hearted cunning and called a coward, so that he betook himself into a wide, hollow place under the tree, and said more than one long prayer against the wickedness of all deceitful guile.

The wolf is to be pitied, and Bishop Ashbourne was to be pitied, too, when he put on his new apron, for, instead of filling his belly by means of it, he found – just as the wolf had done – that it brought him into sad trouble, and only permitted him to pray.

The Bishop's marriage came about in this wise. Miss Agnes Pettifer's particular friend and relation happened to be Miss Cockett, already engaged to Canon Dibben, a lady known at the Palace, and when Miss Cockett received a card of invitation to the Bishop's garden-party – the first in his reign over the diocese – that happened in June, Miss Cockett took Miss Pettifer along with her, for the card of invitation included 'and friends'.

When one chances to look down oneself at a party, and sees that one's garments are a little disordered, one fancies that the eyes of all the world are fixed upon the disarrangement, whether one's shoelace is untied, one's collar unfastened, or one's braces broken.

No one – in or out of a palace – could have been more exact or particular about his person than Bishop Ashbourne. The very idea of untidiness he deprecated and condemned with his whole soul. He had never omitted to say, when he held – as he did once a fortnight – a special service for young men, that a sloven is Anti-Christ. He also observed to his attentive hearers that a man who allowed his trousers to hang bulgingly at the knees is in danger, at any moment, of being a wilful sinner.

It was when the Bishop noticed that Miss Pettifer's eyes were fixed strangely upon him that he discovered that something was wrong.

Toward the further end of the fine Palace lawn, upon the velvet surface of which the guests were strolling in twos and threes, or else resting upon the chairs provided by the butler, Mr Williams – who strangely enough had given notice that very morning, though no one knew why – there was a large plane tree in which the bees buzzed cheerfully.

The Bishop feared to go indoors, for to do so he would have to pass many of his lady guests, so he left the company of Canon Dibben –

with the excuse that he wished to speak to the gardener about the strawberries that ought to have been provided for tea – and retired softly behind the plane tree.

He was followed by Miss Pettifer. At a large garden-party – when it isn't the king's – where everyone goes with one idea, and that only to eat cucumber sandwiches, the guests, of course, spend their time in talking about one another. And suppose that two – a male and a female – happen to turn aside into a little arbour or covered walk or go behind a tree, their departure – and especially if it be rather sudden – is sure, in a moment, to be the talk of the whole garden. At the Bishop's everyone all but pointed with their thumbs at the plane tree. They coughed, winked, and wondered.

Of what exactly happened behind that tree, an author, who himself knows how to blush, would prefer to remain silent. But something must be told. Miss Pettifer, it seems, discovered somewhere amongst her clothes a little pin, with which she must have – for the pin was there and scratched his hand when he undressed – fastened his apron. They waited hidden for a while, but before they left the kindly shelter of the tree, the good man asked the lady to be his wife, and was accepted.

They were married in London, and the pair went abroad.

Even a honeymoon with Miss Pettifer doesn't last for ever, and one day – the exact date was, we think, the tenth of August – the Bishop and his lady returned to the Palace at Portstown. The housekeeper, Mrs Wills, met them at the door, to welcome them on their return, but no sooner did she see Mrs Ashbourne and exchange a word or two with her about the preparations that had been made, than Mrs Wills withdrew to her own room and packed her boxes. She left the next day.

The butler had already gone, having felt, even upon the morning before the garden-party, that there was trouble in the air.

There are some ladies – and Mrs Ashbourne was one of them – who never notice their servants unless to scold them, until they go. Mrs Ashbourne walked the Palace like an inspector, and in every place that she went she found something that was wrong, and looked for a maid to blame for it. The servants all collected in the hall, like swallows in October, and prepared themselves for flight.

On the third day after Bishop Ashbourne brought home his bride, Mrs Ashbourne awoke rather late. She had spent half the night in considering how she could get the better, in a little talk that she would have with her the next day, of the housemaid, Miss Mary.

Mrs Ashbourne opened her eyes; she awoke in a rage, for no one had called her. She knew that the hour was late. Her husband had already gone to the cathedral, where the Holy Communion was to be celebrated at eight o'clock. Bishop Ashbourne had awakened her when he went into his dressing-room to fetch a towel for his bath, but she had dropped off to sleep again, expecting to be called in a few minutes. She now lay, angry and still, and all the house was as still as she.

All at once her stillness left her. She leaped from her bed and rang the bell. There was no reply. Mrs Ashbourne dressed in a hurry, forgetting to pray, and went downstairs. The house was empty, not a creature, not a mouse did she find anywhere.

When the good Bishop returned, hungry after administering the blessed sacrament to a score of pious and elderly ladies, who are wise to listen to such pleasant and comforting words, he found his wife dressed in her outgoing clothes and taking her umbrella from the stand.

'I am going to the town-crier,' she exclaimed fiercely.

Bishop Ashbourne, unlike most of those whose trade is to pray, prayed always from his heart, and though he was not now beside the altar, yet as it were to calm something – some noise that seemed troublesome – he prayed yet again, 'We beseech thee to accept this our bounden duty and service — '

But his wife cut him short.

'Go at once and light the kitchen fire,' she said, 'while I go to the town-crier and order him to call back our servants.'

When Mrs Ashbourne returned, she found her husband had burnt a pile of his latest sermons, but the kitchen fire was not yet lit.

13   MR TRUGGIN AT TEA

SOMETIMES Mr Truggin would grow depressed, though not often. If there were no Tadnol funeral for many months, he would begin to look mournfully at his spade and scratch his head, for he feared that Death had forgotten Tadnol.

''E be grown,' Mr Truggin would say to himself, 'a little forgetful and lazy, and if I have not got 'im to think of, I fear I must remember God, whose ways be funny.'

Mr Truggin thought upon those ways. That God should spy so closely into a sinner's doings had always been a mystery to Truggin, as it had once been to Job. But when he thought the matter over, comparing himself with God – as a discreet man would – Truggin decided that God's spying ways were like his own.

'God,' he told himself, 'must know as well as Tommy Toole – if not better – the difference between Nellie and Betty Spenke. He would never,' considered Truggin, 'be forever spying and looking – where most folks would be ashamed to gaze – unless He enjoyed it.

'And yet,' thought Truggin, 'those that do affirm that God be such a wonderful looker, may not understand what true looking be. He has looked for a very long time,' reflected Truggin, 'at all that goes on upon earth, and for a good reason: He has been searching, amongst man's doings, for some joy to give to him. He do see what men practise, which bain't happiness, and so at last 'E do point out to all where everlasting joy may be found – in a grave.'

'Folk be healthy here,' said Truggin sadly, one Sabbath morning to John Card over his garden hedge.

'I am glad of it,' replied John, 'for bain't it a pleasure to eat a good Sunday dinner and then to step up to Johnnie Toole's, with a well-filled belly and a shilling to spend? That be kindness; but to be attacked suddenly with pain, to lie a-wondering, to gasp and gutter like a candle, to go out in a stink, to be put under dirt for evermore, be another matter.'

Truggin regarded John Card with a deep contempt.

'I fear,' he said, after he had looked at him for a moment, 'that thee haven't been keeping the best of company lately, John. I have heard folk say that thee 've been talking to Mr Dibben, who do speak evil of the living. And Mr Dibben, who do speak evil of the living, bain't likely to speak well of the dead.'

'But who do want to die?' said John Card. 'When Death do take all; 'tain't nice to have all took away.'

Mr Truggin was grieved. Such ideas pained him.

'Thee be mistaken, John,' he said, 'and thee do hurt thee's best friend, talking as thee do, for Death bain't one that do take, 'e be one that do give.'

'Not to I, I hope,' said John.

'Not yet,' observed Truggin, 'but I did once hear Death a-talking.'

'And what did Death say?' asked John Card, stepping back a little.

''E were talking about meself,' replied Truggin modestly. '"Poor, dear Truggin," Death did say, "must be given something – a great king, same as I be, can't let poor Truggin live always without a present. And what hurt do I do to stifle two or three Tadnol folk in a twelvemonth?"'

'But thee's own self, Mister Truggin,' inquired Card, with a wink, 'bain't thee never going to die theeself?'

'Not while I be living,' replied Truggin.

It was Mr Truggin's custom to rise at seven in the morning. He slept – as he had always done – in his shirt, but he was not able to dress as quickly as he used to do when he was younger, because Blacksmith Croot had advised him to wear flannel drawers.

'Thee's two legs will be warmer,' Croot had told him, 'and thee will drink the better so.'

But Truggin had never got quite used to them. He would often forget them altogether, until Mrs Truggin happily suggested his keeping them on all night. And so Truggin came to look at his legs for five minutes each morning to see how warm they were with his drawers on.

Besides the pleasure that he took in his flannel drawers, Truggin also enjoyed looking at the clods of earth when he dug in the Rectory garden. There was something warm about them, too, something that reminded him of his drawers. Whether the clods dwelt in the church-yard and mingled with sandstone rock, or whether their abode was the dampest corner of the Rectory garden, where the ash tree grew, wherever clods were, Truggin thought of them as comfortable and friendly things – like flannel drawers.

Thursday came, the day before Lottie Truggin was to go – as God had advised her – to visit the Bishop in the place of Mr Dottery. Mr Truggin, who had felt more than usually pleased with himself that day, came home in the evening, slowly, for he had been delayed in his journey, with something in each of his pockets.

He had been turning over clods – his favourite pastime – and now he smiled. For to walk with something hidden in your pockets, that you alone know the existence of, and alone know what is there, enhances the joy of the return.

Truggin came to the tea-table with a complacent look that bordered upon jollity. He sat down at the table. In front of him was Lottie, who had been permitted by Mrs Taste – because of her journey the next day – to take tea with her grandparents.

Country people look at one another to see where their hands are. If a farmer meets his servant with his hand behind him, the man is most likely taking home something that does not belong to him.

'What be hiding in they pockets?' asked Mrs Truggin of her husband.

'Nothing,' replied Truggin, with a grin.

He took out one hand and opened it. The hand contained ten shillings. He gave the money to Lottie.

'Mr Dottery,' he said, 'did send 'ee a pound to obey God wi'.'

'But here be only ten shillings,' replied Lottie.

'Of all moneys that be given here,' said Truggin loudly, 'one half be mine.'

Lottie pouted.

Truggin drew out from his other pocket a large potato. He laid the potato down beside his plate, and regarded it with a pleased silence. He laid it there for a particular purpose. He wished the two women to look at it well before he spoke. It was his right, as the master of the house, to command attention. What he brought home to show had always a meaning, and female minds, he knew, need a pointer.

Mr Truggin had brought home the potato as a warning. The potato was a curious one. Besides its monstrous size – and that was enough to astonish any simple person who did not know the ways of Nature –

there was an excrescence upon it, shaped like a nose. This Mr Truggin now pointed at.

''Tis Mrs Ashbourne's,' he said.

Lottie laughed.

'There be some heathen folk,' observed Truggin, holding up his potato and regarding it with a vast admiration, 'that do not recognise the great when they see them, but I be different, and 'tain't only their clothes that I do look at.'

'What be 'en, then?' asked Lottie coyly.

'What I do see do bide in me own imagination,' replied Truggin proudly.

'Thee don't see nothing wicked, I hope?' inquired Lottie.

'No,' replied Truggin, 'but I be one to look under the earth rather than above it, and when Mrs Ashbourne do come happily to be buried – for I wouldn't wish her to live always – thik nose that do show so fine in a potato will feed some poor worm.'

'I shall dream of that,' said Lottie uneasily.

''Tain't only she's nose,' continued Truggin, who sometimes copied in his talk the sermon delivery of the Reverend Silas Dottery, 'all folk be best buried, women, men, and potatoes, and they that be rude above be kind below.'

'Oh!' cried Lottie, 'I would rather have rudeness here than that kindness.'

''Tis always a change for the better, to go,' said Truggin haughtily, 'and when Mrs Ashbourne do come to be buried, she will have to learn better manners from the clay, for all true kindness do begin underground. But what be you?' asked Truggin, looking at Lottie.

'A maiden, I believe,' replied Lottie, with a blush.

'A willing girl,' said Truggin loudly, 'should be behind every old tree. There be large elms that grow high in our village. Some be hollow – within 'tis like a grave – where two can bide happy. If manners bain't learned in a grave, a tree will teach them.

'Bide still,' said Truggin grandly, as though he spoke to some invisible presence, 'and I will tell 'ee all that Mr Dottery has taught me, and then you will be the wisest maid in the world. But who be thee who be so near, for a hollow tree don't tell no names. Thee be pretty; thee's hair, 'tis a light colour, thee's body be pleasant, but wi' me hands in me pockets, how be I to know if thee be Nellie or Betty?'

'Only Tommy Toole do know that,' said Lottie, 'and thee's talk be foolish.'

14   THE RECTORY CUPBOARD

TOMMY TOOLE, a boy of good parts, with fine curly hair, had been brought up wisely. He had always been allowed to do what he wished, so long as what he did he did well. But, as his wishes had not gone far, he had learned no trade, other than to serve his father's customers with beer and tobacco.

Tommy was but a simple boy, though a handsome one. The people of Tadnol looked upon him as a prodigy, a wonder. He had, as everyone knew, a kind of second sight – an intuition – for he knew the difference between things that other people would be likely to suppose were exactly alike.

Even Mr Dottery knew – for a matter of this consequence Truggin would be sure to narrate – all about Tommy's cleverness.

''Tis a kind of learning,' Truggin had informed his master, 'that, without long words, be very cunning.'

'I have no doubt of it,' replied Mr Dottery.

'There mid be two books,' said Truggin, 'whose covers be alike, and how be we to know which be *Robinson Crusoe* and which be *What Katy Did*, when no name bain't writ on cover?'

'You would have to open them,' replied Mr Dottery innocently, 'in order to find out.'

'No one don't say poor Tommy do do that,' said Truggin.

Tommy had ever been – for they were the same age – the happy companion of Nellie and Betty Spenke, the twin daughters of Farmer Spenke who lived at the church farm.

When the girls were infants, upon the day when they were

72

christened by Mr Dottery, their mother tied a pink ribbon round the arm of one, and a blue ribbon round the arm of the other, to know them apart. Thus for three months she knew which was which. But a day came when Mrs Spenke forgot to tie the ribbons, and she would call either of them whichever name came into her head first, for they were both the same thing to her.

The girls grew older, and one day the little boy, Tommy Toole, said to Mrs Spenke, 'Saint Susanna must know which be Betty and which Nellie. Once a vision came to Miss Mary, and if I do go down to the river, Saint Susanna will be sure to tell me which be Betty.'

'Take they brats along too, and drown 'em,' cried Mrs Spenke, who was cross that morning.

Before they reached the river Tommy had quite forgotten what they had come there to do. The three children ran down to the water, very gay and full of chatter.

'We will play at being little fish,' the twins cried, 'and Tommy will catch us.'

The girls took off their shoes and stockings.

'Thee bain't real fish,' said Tommy, looking upon them disdainfully, 'for fish be naked.'

'Fish we will be,' cried the girls, and pulled off their clothes. They splashed in the water happily under the guardian care of Saint Susanna, whose virgin presence haunted the stream, and who played with the children. Saint Susanna took care of them, and so did little Tommy Toole, who waded into the river after them, being always careful to drive these pretty fish into the shallows.

Once when they were near danger and cried out with fright, Tommy took one in his arms and carried her to the bank, and then the other. And before they began to dress again, Tommy Toole called them by their right names.

When all three were safely back at the farm again – for Tommy was always a welcome visitor there – Mrs Spenke discovered that one of the girls had left her shoes behind, though each had them off in the house.

'Whose shoes be lost,' cried Mrs Spenke angrily, 'Nellie's or Betty's? Which be you who have lost they new shoes? Be thee Nellie?' she shouted, looking at the girl who looked most guilty.

Mrs Spenke raised her hand to strike.

'I would give a shilling,' she said, 'to anyone who would tell they maids apart.'

Tommy Toole blushingly held out his hand, and pointed to the other child.

'Thik be Nellie,' he said, 'and there be Betty, pulling the kitten's tail.'

Mrs Spenke boxed both their ears.

'I shall know them for the present,' observed Mrs Spenke, 'but when I do forget I'll send for you, Tom.'

'But I only know them in the river,' said Tommy.

'How did you find out?' asked Mrs Spenke.

'Saint Susanna told me,' answered Tommy ...

With such a secret as this kept safely to himself, it is easy to believe that Tommy Toole was regarded at Tadnol as something very much out of the common. But, being set apart, as one who has a deeper insight than most, Master Tommy was also looked upon in Tadnol a little suspiciously. And so, when Tommy grew older and wished to go out to work, and asked Farmer Spenke to give him employment, he received an evasive answer to his request.

'Those who do know more than other folk do about some maidens,' said the farmer, 'bain't fit for common work: they be too learned.'

'But I bain't learned,' replied Tommy, 'and I can work as well as anyone.'

'I know thee be clever,' remarked the farmer, 'for when our Betty and Nellie do get mixed in their names, thee do put they right.'

'Oh, that bain't nothing,' said Tommy; 'and only last night I dreamed that I worked in a palace.'

'And they two silly maids did dream the same,' replied the farmer, 'but as I bain't nor king nor bishop, thee'd best walk away.'

There are some states of the human mind that men regard with dislike, that are both beneficent and kindly – and melancholy is one of them.

A mild melancholy is a state of felicity, and a safe shield against all base acts and doings. 'Tis the best end to man's days of labour and sorrow – the holy peace that passeth man's understanding, the sabbath rest.

The state of mild melancholy causes all the moods that torment the mind to become still. Thought is calmed by that Holy Oil and utterly freed from the lust of tumult that brings all things to trouble. Resignation rules. In its temple the aisles and cloisters are built of plain earth. Within these are those who have renounced all movement, except the movement that exists in the temple itself.

For there is a movement in the rhythm of melancholy that releases the soul from all knowledge of her former torments, and gives, instead, a studied weariness of life – a weariness that would rather rest where God's hand covers the couch, than be hurried on by lust or fear to uneasy travel.

Mr Dottery communed thus with himself in the stillness of the Rectory study.

He had often before praised a certain kind of melancholy that a scholar, being unworldly, may easily be led to, guided to those pleasant walks by many who have come before him.

'There is in heavenly rest a perfect freedom from all evils.'

Mr Dottery sipped his wine.

'How often do we look within the best and rarest books and find nothing, or, at the most, only a kind of other self thinking, that is seeking – as we are seeking – to rest only.

'To die,' considered Mr Dottery, 'is, in some ways, to be put in motion again, though all good men pray that this should not be so. But at least the swift passage of time might be taught to circle inwards before the last hour comes, so that when that hour does come, there is nothing left to wish for; and as the living had wished, so the dead might consummate.'

Mr Dottery rose and listened. The hour was twelve.

Something was, he thought, in his room as well as himself. He even fancied that the cupboard door opened and shut. He went to the window, opened it, and looked out. The night was very mild. Something passed by him, went into the garden, and disappeared amongst the trees.

A vixen barked on the heath.

Mr Dottery shivered. He sat down again in his chair, finished his glass, and looked at the great study cupboard. Somehow or other the fox's bark had reminded him of Mrs Dibben.

Mr Dottery smiled. Truggin had told him that in diverse places Mrs Dibben had affirmed, in the hearing of one or two sober matrons, that the Rector of Tadnol kept a live girl hidden in his cupboard.

The cupboard was certainly large enough to hold a girl, and there had always been a mystery as to what was inside it. Mr Dottery had once told Mrs Taste that the cupboard was dangerous, and that he did not wish anyone to open it. The cupboard was not locked, but no one in Mr Dottery's household would ever open what he bid them keep closed.

Not even Lottie Truggin had opened it, though she had often wondered what was there, and had once or twice gone so far as to think that there might be some truth in Mrs Dibben's idea. Lottie bided her time. If there were a young woman inside, one day she would be sure to catch her.

Often after midnight, beside a warm fire, with wine on the table, one's thoughts go back to the past. While Mr Dottery had the cupboard in his mind – for he still looked at it – he remembered how, as a young man, before he took orders, he would spend his vacations boating and fishing in the sea. He had become an expert fisherman with net, rod, and line, and possessed all the necessary gear that goes with the sea-fishing craft, and often caught – much to the envy of the trading fishermen of the little village, where he used to stay – great fish with great hooks.

But to look so far back, and after midnight too, made the present the more fleeting, and the future hours, Mr Dottery knew, would as soon come and as soon go. Mr Dottery sighed. He remembered how once he had hooked and landed in his boat a small shark. How well he could recollect how proudly he brought the fish ashore!

Mr Dottery drained another glass. He stepped softly into the hall, after putting out the lamp. Perhaps there was something hidden in the study. The gear of past days that would never be days again.

Mr Dottery's eyes grew moist. He went to bed.

15   BISHOP ASHBOURNE SPOILS A BREAKFAST

THOUGH a bishop is generally believed to be clever in some things, no thinking person would expect him to be clever in all. Bishop Ashbourne found always, to his sorrow, that the laying and the lighting of a fire was a far harder task than to discover, from An Alternative Table of Lessons, as it is printed in the *Common Prayer Book*, the correct portion of the Scriptures to read upon any proper day.

Alas! a good man often thinks that certain ways of life can never alter.

Bishop Ashbourne had always supposed that household servants must ever be as constant and as regular in their service, and in their rising and setting, as the sun and the moon. As the sun generally rose early, so, he knew, the cook rose too. And as the sun moved in the daytime, and the stars at night, so the Bishop was aware that the housemaids and the other members of his family would move according to the kitchen clock across the field of his vision, some carrying things in and some carrying things out of the dining-room.

His servants had always behaved like that, and all their duties had been so correctly performed that the only matter left to the good Ashbourne, who had always had means, was the harmless trouble of paying them – and that, of course, he did through his housekeeper.

Never in his life, since a wise nurse had taught him good manners, had Bishop Ashbourne considered it possible that a cessation of the moving, friendly creatures who did all the work of the house could occur. Once or twice, coming downstairs a little earlier than usual, before he was married – for he liked to rise when he woke – he had chanced to pass a respectable young woman with a brush in her hand, who was sweeping. He had always said to her, 'Good morning, my dear.'

Bishop Ashbourne never thought that there could be anything wrong in that, merely calling a maid 'my dear'. For he said it only, and just in the same manner, as he would have said 'our dear sister' had he been reading over her The Order for the Burial of the Dead, which office is not to be used for any that die unbaptized, or excommunicate, or have laid violent hands upon themselves.

When the servants all left the Palace, the Bishop could not help wondering what he had done to be so used. He put all the blame upon himself. He must, he feared, have done something or other to offend the servants. Perhaps the housemaid, Mary, had not liked him calling her his dear, the first day after he had brought his wife home. He might even have said 'My dear Mary' upon that occasion. He ought never, he thought, have been so eager to get up early that unlucky day.

Bishop Ashbourne and his wife were now quite alone in the great house. The Bishop did what was in his power to do. He rose at five, and after a long time of patient endeavour, during which he would repeat to himself a round dozen of Occasional Prayers, he lit the kitchen fire. After that was done he hardly knew what he did, trying only with the best will, and the utmost patience, to do all that his wife told him, as well as at times during the day to transact the more pressing business of his diocese.

On the Friday morning, the day when he had, at the instigation of his wife, commanded Mr Dottery to come before him, Bishop

BISHOP ASHBOURNE SPOILS A BREAKFAST

Ashbourne had tried in vain to cook an omelette for breakfast. The attempt had failed completely, and the odour of spoilt eggs and butter, and a badly burnt frying-pan, showed how utter and dismal had been the failure.

It was then that Mrs Ashbourne came down to breakfast. She had waked, alas! in a sad temper, for her marriage had not been to her all that she had hoped it would. She had wished to rule a multitude, and she ruled but one man.

Mrs Ashbourne stamped with her foot, she spoke sharply.

'Unless you get me a maid,' she cried, 'I will leave the house too.'

The Bishop did not reply, he only prayed, 'Heavenly Father, who alone makest men to be of one mind in a house, grant to all of us grace, that we may lead a quiet and peaceable life in all godliness and honesty; through Jesus Christ our Lord.'

Bishop Ashbourne spread for himself a slice of bread and butter. He ate a little, and then said cheerfully to his wife:

'You remember Tadnol, my dear, there must be servants there.'

'You mean she, who disgraced the Church by being the only one at the Confirmation,' replied Mrs Ashbourne angrily.

'No,' said the Bishop, 'I was not thinking of the candidate, but I merely recollected that Mrs Dibben told you, just when I burnt my finger with the kettle yesterday, that Farmer Spenke had two daughters, twins, ripe for service.'

Mrs Ashbourne finished her breakfast in a hurry. She went away to dress herself, came back into the kitchen and saw her husband smile.

'You are My Lord, and may well make a mock of me who am but a plain lady.'

KINDNESS IN A CORNER

The Bishop looked at her.

'Deal kindly with the young women,' he murmured.

Mrs Ashbourne went out in a rage.

16 LOTTIE TRUGGIN AT THE PALACE

As soon as his wife was gone, Bishop Ashbourne attended to his affairs. He worked assiduously, and when one o'clock came he found himself to be very hungry, and wished to fry a chop and potatoes for dinner. Such meats, he knew, were in the larder.

Bishop Ashbourne took up the frying-pan, but put it down again sorrowfully. The pan was in no case to be used again, unless carefully cleaned.

The Bishop shook his head, and knowing not what else to do, he could only pray. He prayed aloud.

'O God, our heavenly Father, who by Thy blessed Son hast taught us to ask our daily bread of Thee ... ' and continued to the prayer's end. Alas! no answer came, he received no seasonable relief. But he did not despair. Perhaps, he thought, he had lacked that faith in a prayer that brings a sure answer?

There was the frying-pan, blackened and burnt, a hypocritical mocker in his feast. What could he do with it? Never had he wished more heartily for a good meal. He might have been John Wesley who had ridden sixty miles before breakfast, he felt so hungry. It was hard, indeed, that he would have to be satisfied with plain bread and butter. He prayed the same prayer again even more fervently.

Bishop Ashbourne had only just risen from his knees when there came a ring at the front-door bell.

'Mr Dottery,' cried the Bishop, and went to open the door. But it was not Mr Dottery who stood upon the Palace steps – it was Lottie Truggin.

The Bishop recognised her at once, for, although the large veil that she had worn had partly concealed her features at the Tadnol Confirmation, yet Bishop Ashbourne had regarded her then so earnestly, and had kept what he could see of her in his mind – in order to remember her in his prayers – that he now said, without any hesitation, 'The candidate from Tadnol.'

'God has sent me,' said Lottie, 'in the place of Mr Dottery.'

Bishop Ashbourne remembered the ravens.

'Can you,' he asked, blushing deeply, 'can you clean a frying-pan that's been badly burnt?'

'Oh yes,' answered Lottie, 'I can do that, if its bottom bain't out.'

'Good,' said the Bishop eagerly, 'and can you fry a mutton chop and potatoes?'

'Are the potatoes sliced?' asked Lottie.

'I hope not,' said the Bishop, crossing himself.

'But they should be,' replied Lottie, 'after they are peeled.'

Bishop Ashbourne led her hurriedly into the kitchen. He showed her the frying-pan.

''Twill come off,' said Lottie, 'though 'twas a fool that did it.'

'Why, so it was,' laughed the Bishop, and showed her the larder.

As soon as Lottie took charge of the cooking, the Bishop sat himself down in the cook's easy-chair and began to take notes for a sermon that he was to preach before the king of England on the following Sunday. He soon lost himself in his task, forgetting all about Lottie and about what she was doing, for he had chosen this as his text, 'No man can serve two masters.'

Bishop Ashbourne had just completed the final note for his sermon, begging all men to be kind and loving to one another – and especially kings – when Lottie told him that the luncheon was cooked.

She had certainly done wonders. All was laid out in the manner that Bishop Ashbourne had been used to before the servants left.

'And who taught you to cook, my dear?' asked the Bishop, shaking the crumbs out of his napkin into the fire, when he had well eaten.

'Mrs Taste,' replied Lottie, 'and she once even allowed me to make an omelette.'

'Show me how,' asked the Bishop, 'for I did not use all the eggs.'

He watched Lottie with interest.

'This is indeed a seasonable relief,' he said to himself.

They divided the omelette between them.

'Nothing, no, not even that manna that God Himself cooked in heaven, could be done better,' observed the Bishop when he had finished his share.

In reply Lottie moved her chair from the table, came to Bishop Ashbourne, and knelt before him. The Bishop looked at her gratefully.

'You don't wish to be confirmed again, surely?' he asked.

'No,' answered Lottie, 'I only kneel to ask a blessing for myself, and forgiveness for Mr Dottery.'

The Bishop remembered why God is good – because He is merciful.

'The Blood of our Lord Jesus Christ,' he prayed, 'which was shed for thee, preserve thy body and soul unto everlasting life.'

'And Mr Dottery?' asked Lottie, still on her knees.

'The peace of God be with him,' prayed the Bishop, 'and with his people, Amen.'

Lottie rose happily.

'I must go now,' she said.

'Won't you help me to wash up?' asked the Bishop anxiously.

'Oh, your wife can do that,' laughed Lottie.

They smiled upon one another. Lottie turned, made a merry gesture at the Bishop with her fingers, and ran out of the house.

She had not been gone five minutes, before Mrs Ashbourne returned, and found her husband sitting before a great kitchen fire, busy writing his sermon from the notes that he had made.

'You have lunched?' said she.

'Never better in my life,' answered Bishop Ashbourne.

'Who has been here?' inquired Mrs Ashbourne, sniffing suspiciously.

'Only the confirmed candidate,' replied the Bishop, 'who cooked the lunch.'

'Where is she?' cried Mrs Ashbourne, looking about her angrily.

'Gone,' said the Bishop, beginning to write again with his quill pen. 'We left the washing-up for you, and Lottie said you were to be sure to remember to use a little soda for the frying-pan.'

Mrs Ashbourne changed colour, her pale face grew red.

'You had a cook here and never kept her for me,' she exclaimed fiercely. The Bishop looked up, troubled. 'You ought to have tied her up,' cried his wife.

'I gave her my blessing, and forgave Mr Dottery,' said the Bishop; and he inquired gently how his wife had got on.

'I called at Mrs Dibben's,' said she, for however angry a woman is, she always likes to talk. 'Mrs Dibben walked to Tadnol with me. We walked over that horrid heath.'

'God made it,' murmured the Bishop.

'And Sarah Dibben told me all the dreadful doings of Mr Dottery, how he keeps — '

Bishop Ashbourne held up his hand.

'I have pardoned him,' he said in a tone of authority; and then added more mildly, 'He keeps pigs, I believe.'

'At Farmer Spenke's,' continued Mrs Ashbourne angrily, 'I saw the girls who want places.'

'And engaged them, I hope?' said the Bishop anxiously.

'They are twins,' observed Mrs Ashbourne, 'and are exactly alike, so I said to the woman, the mother, "If one were cook and the other the housemaid, how should I know them apart?" "You never would," laughed the mother rudely. "But I must," I said, "for otherwise I should be always finding fault with the wrong one; for the servant in the kitchen might not be the cook." One of the girls laughed. "Tommy Toole knows the difference between us," she said naughtily. "But only when we are alone with him in a corner," sniggered the other. I called them two drabs.'

'And withdrew, I hope,' said Bishop Ashbourne, a little sadly.

'I went away,' replied the lady.

Mrs Ashbourne clenched her fist. 'I have tried,' she shouted, 'and now it is your turn, you must get me Lottie Truggin. Go to Tadnol and entice her away. Offer her every good thing that you can think of. Show her every kindness, give her laces and ribbons, tell her you will hold up your skirts and dance before her, if she will come.'

The Bishop smiled.

'I could hardly do that,' he replied, 'for perhaps my Lord of Canterbury might think me immodest.'

'Fiddle-de-dee!' said the lady; 'pray, what has he to do with Lottie Truggin?'

'He has everything to do with her,' answered the Bishop. 'Lottie belongs to the Church of England; she has been baptized and confirmed.'

'Once too often,' sneered Mrs Ashbourne.

Mrs Ashbourne looked very grim. She had made up her mind what to tell him to do.

'In your spare time,' she said, 'when you are not working as my servant, and when you have none of your other foolery to do, you must go in disguise to Tadnol and find a way to get Lottie – or else those Spenke girls – to come to us.'

'I will try what I can do,' replied the Bishop humbly; and taking out a little knife from his pocket, he began to mend his pen.

17   A BISHOP'S LETTER

'HOW curious it is,' mused Mr Dottery, 'when one considers it, in how many odd directions we move our fingers.'

He had just finished breakfast, and had let the key of his letter-bag slip under the table, and so knelt down to search until he had found it.

'Did Jesus,' he wondered, 'when He was a little boy, find the mother of Joseph sweeping the house to look for that piece of money? Perhaps He found it Himself.'

Mr Dottery picked up the key. He remembered, a little uncomfortably, how in going down to the cellar the day before to fetch a bottle of wine, his candle went out and he was left in darkness. As he groped about, where he supposed the right bottle to be, he put his fingers into a nest of cockroaches.

Mr Dottery now unlocked the letter-bag and peeped into it cautiously – 'Was there an adder there?'

He saw only one letter.

Mr Dottery looked into his cup. There was a little coffee left, and this he drank slowly.

He set down his cup, took the letter out of the bag and broke the seal. Mr Dottery laid the letter beside his plate; he was in no hurry to read it. Instead of opening the letter, he took up the cream jug. Finding cream there, he poured himself out another cup of coffee.

When that was done, he took the letter out of the envelope, and read the contents.

KINDNESS IN A CORNER

THE PALACE, PORTSTOWN
November 7th 1920

DEAR BROTHER IN CHRIST, Some time ago I was much pained to hear from Canon Dibben – as I wrote then to inform you – that he charged you with being somewhat remiss in the proper governance of your cure. I then most mildly invited you to come and visit me, so that we might talk over, as two brothers in the same glorious hope should, the complaint of the Canon's. You came not; but neither our expectations nor our ways are God's.

I have heard my nurse say to me when I was a child – and I have, alas! of late often put this proverb to an unhappy test – that the proof of the pudding's goodness is in the eating thereof. And you, dear Mr Dottery, no doubt wishing – and most praiseworthily – to show me a dish of your own making, one, I mean, taught by you and trained in the good ways of your own kitchen, sent to me – to plead against the suspicions that Canon Dibben has told me of – a young woman, whose kindness of heart is only equalled by the curious cunning and nimbleness of her fingers.

In your gentle counterfeit – for in the presence of Lottie, I could perceive you yourself – 'twas shown me, by God's especial grace, that even a Canon may be sometimes mistaken. For many of us that are churchmen do show sometimes more righteous zeal than wise discretion. And in our eager hurry to reach after the good and to destroy the evil, we sometimes slip and fall. 'Tis better to pray than to judge.

I need hardly tell you that I am now convinced – for Lottie proved plainly to me – that you teach, as you ever have taught, both by precept and example, Justice, Judgment, and Truth.

A BISHOP'S LETTER

And now, as you have been courteous enough to pay your devoir to me, by your representative, may I also be permitted to pay my court to you? 'The riches and goods of Christians,' as we read in the thirty-eighth Article of our reformed religion, 'are not common, as certain Anabaptists do falsely boast.' If they were, though I would never have the ratification of the Article unratified, we might, perhaps, you and I, share Lottie Truggin between us about luncheon time.

Believe me to be, your ever loving brother in Jesus Christ,

PORTSTOWN

Mr Dottery laid down the letter. There might have been – though a keen eye could hardly have noticed it – a slight movement of Mr Dottery's lips that, had he been any other than himself, one not so sure of the honour due to a high place, were perhaps a smile.

'When the proud Menecrates,' Mr Dottery bethought him, 'had writ a strange letter to Philip of Macedon, he sent back no other answer than this – "I advise you to take yourself off to Anticyra", noting thereby that he was crazed and had much need of a good purge.

'But, alas!' thought Mr Dottery, 'God has certainly sent Lottie, in very truth, to visit the Bishop. Poor man, he is married to Miss Pettifer. Alas! alas! I fear that women are indeed to blame for a great number of misfortunes that fall hard upon us. I fear that Mrs Ashbourne is too busy concerning those things that a woman can never perfectly understand, so that the poor Bishop is compelled, by her ill-judged behaviour, to take her place and to talk only of pies and puddings.

'At Tadnol, thank goodness, there is no woman who resembles Miss Pettifer. Here they do not scatter themselves abroad for purposes of folly, while the husband, who would much rather lead his mild spouse to God, has instead to bake and brew. What decent woman would allow, to her everlasting shame, a poor man to peel onions?

'It is pleasant,' considered Mr Dottery, 'to think of these Tadnol women. They do not wish to embarrass God by considering His terrible ways too closely, and they never care to listen to Canon Dibben when he tells them – contrary to Christ's ordinance – that the Sacrament should be reserved, carried about, lifted up or worshipped. Such matters do not interest our country women, who are only concerned – and wisely so – with the multiplicity and preservation of the species.'

Mr Dottery was not surprised at the contents of the Bishop's letter. That Bishop Ashbourne should have seen Lottie Truggin without the Spirit of God whispering to him that He had sent her, he never once doubted. Neither did he doubt that God, great and high though He be, had condescended to give Lottie His commands, though Mr Dottery guessed that when He spoke to her, and told her, in a happy hour, to visit Portstown, He appeared to her – in a vision – exactly like another Tommy Toole.

18   RED HAIR

THERE is hardly ever to be found, living here upon the earth, a human creature who does not wish to touch, to handle, or to probe some mystery that, by the commandment of an all-wise creator, is rightfully hidden.

Even though this is so, all latitude and indulgence should be given to the inquisitiveness of children, which is most right and proper. But when one has reached an adult age – when one's mind should have grown used to the illusory nature of the appearances that are about us – one should ever be so strong in saving grace that, when we see a lovely flower, we should bow before it, knowing it only as a fair vision sprung from an earthy grave to which all beauty returns, without the wish to pluck it from its root, and enjoy for our own selfish delight its soothing fragrance.

When one has learned to pass by beauty, merely pausing for a moment to give God thanks, that He has allowed our mortal eyes to gaze upon immortal loveliness, surely one can pass by, too – for there is nothing that we see that we do not pass by – all ugliness, considering that this is a mystery also of God, as deep as beauty itself.

Thus true piety – the least noticeable and the least to be understood of all the strange endowments of mankind – that is clothed in the garment of solitary meditation, can be bold enough to see what is ugly and what is beautiful, without doing any hurt to either.

'Piety can alone acknowledge, with a becoming grace, the least and the smallest loving-kindness, without wishing to follow the kindness too far down into the hidden places of God's deep love from where the kindness has come.'

Such were the thoughts, one morning, of Mr Dottery, the Rector of Tadnol, but such were not the thoughts of Mrs Dibben, whose name was – before she married – Miss Sarah Amy Cockett.

At Dodder, where the Dibbens lived, all was prying and discovery. Dodder might have been a wide lake, in which those that lived near fished for evil doings, each one trying to catch something with a stronger stench than his neighbour. Indeed, those that looked and fished in Dodder were more than those that did not. The sweetest morning air in May was only breathed in there with the hope that some merry tale – the more gross in detail the better for the hearers – would float by at cockcrow, so that a waiting listener might hear.

Thus, by catching here and there a pretty story, Mrs Dibben did feed herself, and that well, in Dodder, upon what she heard. But the doings of Farmer Greedy in Smock Lane, though well enough to hear of once or twice, became after a while, even to Sarah, a little tedious. Her desires went further afield, even to Tadnol, and lit early upon Mr Dottery.

There, certainly, was a man whose reputation, if she could pull it down, would make a pretty clatter where it fell. Sarah Dibben's judgment of men came from her experience of her husband's conduct in a beech wood. She always regarded Mr Dibben's antics there as the very same manners that any other man would use if, after a sober Lent, properly employed, he were suddenly invited at Easter to dine with Lord Bullman, and afterwards had the duty set him to lead a lady to her home through a wood.

RED HAIR

Though not as a rule interested in the way that Nature builds a grove, at least no more interested than was necessary – for his patron sometimes talked of forestry when the ladies had left the table – yet Mr Dibben, being alone under the trees with a lady, began to inquire of her how trees came, whether or no they grew up from seeds, or from the eager sprouting of their spreading roots. Sarah Cockett replied discreetly that she knew more about mice.

She made sure of him then, for Mr Dibben, whose feelings – when tipsy – could be romantic, laid hands upon her.

No man, indeed, answered so amorously well to good fare as did Mr Dibben. Boiled mutton made him kindly, a roast duck gave him eyes to see that Mrs Dibben moved like a woman, and a glass or two of port wine would cause him to look at the clock to see how the evening sped.

Knowing so much from such a simple pattern beside her, it was quite impossible for Mrs Dibben ever to think of the existence of the Reverend Silas Dottery, without adding to that existence a heavy sin. But, try as she could and listen to all as she did, no breath of scandal – not so much as a whiff – ever mingled Mr Dottery's name with either his faithful housekeeper, or her duteous handmaid, Lottie Truggin.

Though such was the case, Mrs Dibben had early begun to grow suspicious when she heard of the great study cupboard at Tadnol. Everyone knew that there was something inside it. It was known that Mr Dottery had once warned Archdeacon Ford not to lean too heavily against the cupboard door on his way to bed, in case it came open.

Mrs Dibben was sure that such nervousness about this particular possession of Mr Dottery's told a tale. She concluded that there must be something inside that he valued highly, that he did not wish to be seen, that he wished to be hidden.

When once a woman's supicions are afoot, they are soon set a-running. All that is seen comes into the same bandbox, and every little tale that is heard makes more certain the guilt of the suspect.

It happened one evening, rather late, that Mr Dibben, in passing Tadnol Rectory – having been to see his mother who lived at Shelton, but would not die there – saw Mr Dottery's study window open suddenly and something white come out of it. Sounds, too, that were not holy, had often been heard by one and another coming from the Rectory shrubbery.

But, most of all, Mrs Dibben's hopes were aroused by what John Card, who was wont to peep more than ever an honest-minded man should, had once seen. This was nothing else than the vision of a young woman, half hidden in the boughs, at the top of one of the elms in the Rectory garden, while at the bottom stood Mr Dottery begging her to come down.

And that was not all. For Mr Potter of Johnson's Stores affirmed in Mrs Dibben's parlour that, when on his way once to the back door at the Tadnol Rectory, he had seen Mr Dottery kneeling upon his knees, 'to a woman', he supposed.

But whatever were the motives of Mrs Dibben in what she looked for, her husband tried, according to the lights that he had, to do what was proper. He felt for a sinner, knowing that he himself had sometimes done amiss, and prayed for every sinner's forgiveness. He was always eager for the good of the Church in whose bosom he lived.

But he did not know his own weakness, so when his wife told him,

96

as certain truth – with all her own experience of a woman behind her – that it was utterly impossible for Mr Dottery, being a Protestant, to live richly and yet be honest, Canon Dibben could do nothing less than believe her. And when she went on to tell him again – what, she said, all people knew now – that Mr Dottery really kept a young girl hidden in his cupboard, and fed her with wine and apples, Mr Dibben could only feel sure that he had acted rightly in informing against Mr Dottery as regards the management of his village – though he had not known then about the hidden sin.

After a little harmless conversation upon this subject one Sunday shortly after morning prayers, Mrs Dibben said decidedly:

'The little wretch has red hair, and it's believed that she wears garters with a cupid worked in green silk upon each of them. She is also, as that sort of thing most generally is, shockingly and wickedly young. No one could live as she does, nor yet where she lives, who was out of her teens.'

Mr Dibben agreed with a groan. No one, he was sure, could live in a cupboard, and only come out to drop a garter or to climb to the top of a great tree – where, though Mr Dibben was not aware of it, a loose page of proof had been blown by the wind out of Mr Dottery's hand, as he walked in the garden – unless she were under twenty.

'Alas!' said Mrs Dibben, seeing that her husband was moved, and wishing to increase his dolour, 'often, upon a warm summer's night, words of endearment have been heard, even in the road, to come from Mr Dottery's room, such as "vouchsafe to give us", "he that soweth", and "oblation and satisfaction", words that certainly mean the strangest of doings.'

'I fear so,' replied Mr Dibben.

'You must find out the truth, Canon,' said the lady.

'But how?' he asked.

'In this manner,' answered Mrs Dibben: 'you must find a way to get hold of the servant.'

'Alas!' sighed Canon Dibben, 'I fear that Mrs Taste knows nothing about sin; she is too good a cook.'

Mrs Dibben looked at her husband shrewdly.

'You must attempt Lottie Truggin,' she said.

19   MR DOTTERY IS TOLD OF THE WITCH

MR DOTTERY drew his chair nearer to the study table, and gently rubbed his forehead with two fingers. He had forgotten a Latin word that he needed. He was turning, for his own pleasure, the old French of Froissart into Latin, and now he was forced to search for the word that he wanted in a dictionary. This labour was unusual for him, and he feared that his memory was not what it used to be.

He opened the dictionary, but remained for a while inattentive to the lesson he had set himself. The forgetting of that word made him remember his sins. He had done, he knew, sometimes what he should not have done, and at other times had omitted to do what he ought.

Only the evening before he should have held a service, for the season was Advent, but he had not done so. Also Mrs Spenke had sent to him with this rather singular request:

Dear Mr Dottery, We are very much in need of your advice; do come and visit us. I am sure that you cannot refuse, because neither Betty nor Nellie will get up to milk or to feed the pigs, unless someone can tell which of them is to marry Tommy Toole.

Mr Dottery excused himself. And then, after sending a rather short reply to Mrs Spenke, he had spoken a little quickly to Mrs Taste, when she came to tell him that John Card had called to say that the time had come to sweep the study chimney.

'Let another time come,' he had replied.

Mr Dottery, with the dictionary open before him, decided in his mind that he must never let the thought go from him that he had done many wrong things, and that his own unworthiness made him a fit and proper companion for the saddest sinner.

Seeing himself thus, Mr Dottery grew happier. He pushed the dictionary a little to one side, and remembered with pleasure that Lottie's mission had been entirely successful, and that he was relieved of that care. In other matters he would try to do better, and thinking so, there came a knock at the door and Truggin was announced.

There was always something pleasant about the appearance of Truggin when he came from his usual duties to tell his master some news that he thought he should know. Even with his hat off, he would have upon him some sign or other to show that he had been about an earthy business. Did he come in from the digging of a grave, a centipede or a worm sometimes dropped from him, that he would, if possible, crush with his foot before Mr Dottery knew of its presence. Or else, as at this present time, when he had been sweeping leaves, he did not fail to carry two of them into his master's study. These trespassing leaves he carefully picked up, knowing that if he had let them stay upon the carpet, he would afterwards have been blamed for his dirty ways by his granddaughter Lottie.

Mr Dottery invited Truggin to sit down.

'Tell me,' he asked, 'what has happened. Has the ghost of Saint Susanna frightened John Card into saying a prayer, or am I required to christen another child of Mrs Croot's that is likely to die?'

'No one is likely to die,' replied Truggin gloomily, 'and I mid as well go dig a grave for me woon pleasure.'

'Your time will not be wasted,' observed Mr Dottery dryly.

'No, no, for we bain't always here,' said Truggin, more cheerfully. 'But I be come to tell 'ee' – Truggin came nearer to his master and said, in a loud whisper – 'wold Mrs Tubb be come to heath cottage.'

'And who is Mrs Tubb?' asked Mr Dottery.

Mr Truggin went back to his chair and peeped under it, he stepped to the window and looked out, he went to the door and listened, then he returned to his master.

'Mrs Tubb be a witch,' he said.

Truggin looked knowingly at Mr Dottery and shook his head. In that shake of his head he seemed to tell of all the evil doings of witches who had come, one time or another, since the beginning of the world, to dwell at Tadnol, in order to harm poor people.

'Has Mrs Tubb lived long upon the heath?' asked Mr Dottery, smiling.

'She don't live there at all,' replied Truggin, 'but she be there sometimes.'

Mr Dottery wished to hear more, but he did not question Truggin, who always liked to tell a story in his own way.

'Though nothing bain't told of 'en in the Bible,' said Truggin, 'Croot do know, Card do know, and Johnnie Toole do know, that the Devil have been to Portstown and bought a motor-car.'

'Just the very thing that he would buy,' ejaculated Mr Dottery.

'And 'e do carry thik witch to heath cottage in 'en,' whispered Truggin.

'One would expect so,' observed Mr Dottery, 'for now that the kingdom of Satan is so enlarged, and the Devil's subjects have become so rich, no old woman who has sold herself to him would be likely to take so cheap a thing as a broomstick to travel by. And no doubt, the offer of a ride in the Devil's conveyance is a fine bait to a female.'

''Tis true,' said Truggin, who had rather expected his master to disbelieve his story, 'for one night Tommy Toole, being asked which of the Spenke maidens were Betty – for a posted present had come for she – because the moon did shine bright, 'e did take they both out together, so as to make no mistake, for each did say she were Betty.

'They were gone far across the heath – for maids walk fast when they do quarrel – and were come nearly to the witch's cottage, where old Fanny did live before she were happy to die. 'Twas then that the moon were hid under a dark cloud, and they saw, coming along the heath road from Dodder, two great shining eyes.'

'The car lamps, I suppose,' said Mr Dottery.

'Thee 've guessed right,' answered Truggin.

'"Tommy," said one of they maids, "I don't care who I be so long as we do get safe home." The great car came along, and swerved down the grassy track to the heath cottage. The driver's eyes shone worse than the lamps ... Tommy be a brave boy wi' maids.'

'I have no doubt of it,' said Mr Dottery.

'But no sooner,' continued Truggin, 'did he see the Devil carry into heath cottage what do belong to Mrs Tubb, than 'e did call out "Nellie! Betty!" and away they went, as fast as they could run, back to Tadnol. But that bain't all.'

Truggin looked suspiciously into his hat, as if he supposed a witch might be hidden in it.

'What more is there to tell?' asked Mr Dottery.

'Late last night,' replied Truggin, looking nervously at the great study cupboard, 'when I were smoking a new pipe that Lottie had brought me as a present from Portstown — '

Mr Dottery coughed.

' — and holding upon my knees the burial chart of the Tadnol churchyard, that be me favourite reading, for the names of the buried be marked upon each grave, and 'tis nice to read of those who be happy, I was just considering where Croot and Spenke mid like to lie, when a loud knocking came at the door.

'"Let them knock again," I said.

'And so they did, and louder, so that I was forced to open the door a little ways, and I heard a voice in the darkness saying "that she who did bide alone upon the heath wished to see the Tadnol clergyman."'

'But surely, Truggin,' said Mr Dottery, uneasily, 'you gave a good excuse for me, so that I should not have to go. You know well enough that I never like to, and always avoid, if possible, going to see old women.'

'And neither be I one,' replied Truggin, 'who do like to hear strange voices at night-time, and so I did close the door, lock it fast, take out the key, and talked through keyhole.'

'And what did you say?' asked Mr Dottery.

'I did say,' answered Truggin, 'that she'd better send for Canon Dibben, for thee being an old man bain't to be trusted wi' no old woman.'

'Ha! You told her so, did you?' exclaimed Mr Dottery.

'Yes,' replied Truggin, 'for I did wish to save thee a journey.'

'I trust that you contented her and told her no more,' said Mr Dottery.

'Yes,' replied Truggin, 'I did tell more, for I said that, when thee be out visiting, thee do reel to and fro like a drunken man, and are at your wits' ends.'

'I trust that, after hearing that, Mrs Tubb didn't want to see me,' remarked Mr Dottery.

'She did urge you the more to come,' replied Truggin.

'Alas!' said Mr Dottery, 'surely she must have wished to see someone else rather than me?'

Truggin tried to remember.

'Yes,' he replied, 'she did inquire whether anyone else as bad as thee did live in village?'

'And how did you answer that question?' asked Mr Dottery.

'I said,' observed Truggin, 'that they twins be as bad, and then me thought the woman came nearer to the door, and whispered through keyhole, "I do tell all fortunes for a shilling."'

'And you opened the door?' suggested Mr Dottery.

'In the morning,' replied Truggin, 'but the woman was gone.'

20 MR DOTTERY PUTS UP HIS UMBRELLA

M R DOTTERY awoke the next morning with a feeling of love and gratitude in his heart. He had of late, since he was relieved of the trouble of going to Portstown as a prisoner, felt more than ever grateful to the kindness of God that He had vouchsafed to him in the corner where he lived.

Mr Dottery sat up in bed and exclaimed, 'Gloria in excelsis Deo, et in terra pax hominibus.'

Lying down again, he was more than ever conscious of God's love and of his own well-being within. A well-being that went far beyond his bodily needs, showing that, as God is the centre and home of all love and goodness, we that feed upon Him – though but poor sons of Adam – may become a kind of goodness too.

During the few moments that Mr Dottery had lived in Tadnol – for he knew the hours, the days, and the years to be but moments – the village creatures that moved, the men and women, the children budding in a pit, had never done him intentionally, by word or deed, an ill turn, only making those gains by him that a human neighbour will ever make out of a good man.

Mr Dottery had never thought much of what went on about him, only as far as to gaze humanely upon the picture so that his mind might the easier return to his own labours. It was fortunate, and to the credit of the good clay out of which Mr Dottery was formed, that, when he was awakened from his own quiet by a command to travel, the thoughtful kindness of his neighbours was the first thing that he saw.

And so Mr Dottery, who when he walked abroad set one foot always first, having now got out of bed to pray, crept in again for a little, and felt sure that the fiery shapes of terror that elsewhere, in diverse parts of the earth, shame, terrify, and torment, at Tadnol were smoothed and rounded and rendered harmless, as were the pebbles in the river.

And Mr Dottery, too, felt a change in himself, for he knew that a certain assurance had been with him when he first came to Tadnol, because of his learning, and because he had never been troubled by poverty, and that this kind of pride had sometimes made him a little curt with the world.

That was now quite gone. Mr Dottery's heart was opened. There would be now at Tadnol nothing, however small, that he would not take an interest in. He even began to wonder, as he lay in bed, which way the wind was blowing.

At eight o'clock Mrs Taste brought in his hot water – he did not like to take tea so early. Mrs Taste found Mr Dottery reading. She bid him good-morning as was her wont, but hesitated a little in the doorway before she went out.

'Perhaps there is some little matter,' said Mr Dottery, smiling, 'that you would wish to consult me about, Mrs Taste?'

'It's Lottie,' answered Mrs Taste, 'who wishes to carry a rice pudding to Mrs Tubb. Would it be right for me to allow her to go to the heath cottage this afternoon?'

'If you wish her to go, there can be no harm in her going,' replied Mr Dottery.

Mrs Taste still held open the door.

'But Truggin has told me,' she observed hesitatingly, 'that Mrs Tubb talks of nothing but of young girls and of clergymen.'

'And both should be spoken of,' said Mr Dottery. 'In all good companies the clergy should be mentioned, for their lives are meek and their hearts ready to receive the good that God gives. And who would be so great a churl as to prevent young maidens from being the subject of conversation, when it is by their kindness that so many sad ones are made joyful?'

But Mrs Taste still looked anxious.

'The heath's a lonely place,' she observed. 'There are dark hidden corners in it.'

'Angels and archangels, and all the company of the heavens do guard a virgin,' cried Mr Dottery, 'and I myself may walk that way this afternoon.'

'Then Lottie shall go,' said Mrs Taste, closing the bedroom door and going downstairs.

When he had finished his breakfast and was safely settled in his study, the fire burning well, Mr Dottery began to read certain letters of Bishop Hooper – a godly man, once Bishop of Gloucester, and a friend of one Master Theodore – who wrote a book upon our Lord's Sermon on the Mount.

Mr Dottery, liking the matter, translated aloud:

'We know in whom we have believed, and we are sure that we shall lay down our lives in a good cause. Meanwhile aid us with your prayers, that He who hath begun a good work in us will perform it even unto the end. We are the Lord's, let Him do what seemeth good in His eyes.'

Mr Dottery still read, though silently, the noble writing of perse-cuted men which often made his own eyes moist, and he wondered – if he had been hunted to the death by Canon Dibben – how he would have behaved.

All the while that he read, Mr Dottery was aware of a wish to ask a question of someone. As a rule, when he had wished to ask anything, he would go to his books where the question that troubled him would be sure to be discussed, if not explained, but now, though he sought diligently, he could find nothing that satisfied him as a proper reply to his doubt.

Mr Dottery was still reading when the luncheon bell rang, and after that meal was over, he bethought him of his walk upon the heath that afternoon to visit Mrs Tubb, and to ask her a question. But, before he started out, he found a new shilling that he put into his pocket.

The November afternoon appeared, when Mr Dottery looked out of the door, to be mild and friendly, and seemed as simple and quiet in its behaviour as any Tadnol old maid.

'Though I am not the one to trust her,' murmured Mr Dottery, and took his umbrella with him.

He felt unusually light-hearted, and even caught a falling leaf in his hand as he went under an elm tree. The day was very still, and the leaf had fluttered down slowly.

He climbed the little hill that led to the heath, and, once there, he paused upon the dry turf under an oak tree, and gathered a few acorns, putting them into his coat pockets, remembering for the first time that he kept pigs. He noticed, too, other heath matters besides the acorns. The spiders had been busy, and under every damp gorse bush there were shining webs. Mr Dottery bent his head to examine them, and sniffed the pleasant earthy smell that came from the bushes. He remembered that, as a boy, he had liked that cool thick smell.

'A pleasant scent,' he observed.

Though Mr Dottery was a Christian believer, and thought of God, yet – and this may happen to every pious man – he could not be always sure that God thought of him.

'What am I that God should know of me?' he asked himself, kneeling down in the road to watch an ant cross the path. 'When the books are opened this little creature may have a place in heaven, though not I. God passeth by the Archbishop of York, but He speaks to Lottie. I hope He will remember my name. Perhaps He knows me as Silas.'

'How glad I am,' thought Mr Dottery, rising from his knees, 'and how thankful to be only going this short pilgrimage to visit a poor woman. Had I been obliged to go that journey to Portstown, what should I have done had I met a fellow clergyman – not knowing him – and taken him for a footballer?'

Mr Dottery always wore the cloth proper to his profession. He had never willingly deceived anyone in his life, and, being an ordained priest, he had never disguised himself, or walked out with merely an ugly collar as a proof of his ordination. To pretend in the least matter, even in the matter of trousers, to be anything other than what one is, he used to say, 'is an unnecessary sin.'

Mr Dottery had not often walked so far, and he felt a little lonely, having only found companionship in the spiders and one ant. Looking about at the wide spaces, he experienced a kind of pleasure in his heart when he remembered that Lottie Truggin was to walk that way too. He had not gone many steps further when a sound came to him that is easily heard – the laughter of girls.

And so Mr Dottery, who had stepped a little out of the path to climb a small knoll, saw two young women pass along the road in the direction of the witch's cottage.

As they went along Mr Dottery was aware that their merry steps disturbed the spiders, for more than one of these insects hurried into her nest, and remained still until the girls were gone by. And a squirrel, too, looked down from a fir tree when the young women passed under, shook its head, and twicked its tail with some suspicion, as though such monsters might have a naughty wish to steal his nuts, a good store of which were hid in the tree – or else had come there with the unholy and wicked desire to change the heath into a pink frock or a sliced lemon cake.

'Betty and Nellie Spenke,' observed Mr Dottery, to a rabbit that had come out of its hole to look at him, and then correcting himself, 'no, Nellie and Betty Spenke.'

'It is awkward,' he considered, striding to the path again, 'indeed it is, that I never know the difference between those two girls. They both sing in the church choir every Sunday afternoon. I ought to know one from the other, but I fear that, when I pass them in the church path, I always call them by the wrong names. Once,' recollected Mr Dottery, 'when I met them both in the lane with Tommy Toole I asked him to put me right, but he only replied that a matter of such importance could not be decided at a moment's notice.'

Mr Dottery shivered. A cool breath of wind crept over the heath to remind whoever walked there that all men are mortal.

MR DOTTERY PUTS UP HIS UMBRELLA

'I hope a lion has not eaten Lottie,' sighed Mr Dottery.

Mr Dottery was aware at that moment that the heath was darkening and, looking at the sky, he observed that a large cloud that resembled his Greek lexicon – for it looked as black – was close above him. The sun had entirely gone and large drops of rain were beginning to fall.

Mr Dottery put up his umbrella.

He was now come within a few hundred yards of the witch's cottage, that was at the edge of the heath and near to Dodder where Mr Dibben ruled. The heath there had a different look. It seemed to have lost the happy freedom of its way; the very heath tufts and thorn bushes had lost their innocence, as though Canon Dibben had tried to get them to confess their sins. The road was covered with sharp flint stones instead of pretty pebbles made of rainbow colours, and a tree nearby looked blasted and as if the voice of Mrs Dibben had once reached it from the Vicarage beneath.

Mr Dottery turned a little out of his way, quickened his stride, and arrived at the witch's cottage.

This was a very old building, made of mud, and seemed to stand only because it wondered which way to topple. The mud walls were hidden by ivy, and the one window that could be seen had lost its glass and was boarded up. The place, except for wreaths of smoke that arose from the chimney, appeared utterly deserted.

Mr Dottery walked boldly on, and knocked at the door. He knocked three times and, at the third knock, he was invited to enter. He opened the door and went in.

Mr Dottery found himself in a room that appeared to be the whole of the cottage, for above him there were rafters and thatch and below him the stone floor. The place was dark, having no light except the fire, and it was some while before he could distinguish who was there. Growing accustomed to the dim light, Mr Dottery saw a woman, whom he supposed to be Mrs Tubb, standing in a recess near to her chimney, while, sitting together upon a form – as far away as they could get from the witch – were the twin daughters of Mr Spenke.

Mrs Tubb evidently saw Mr Dottery for the first time when he was able to see her, and she pointed out to him a three-legged stool in a corner upon which he immediately sat down.

He was glad to rest, for the walk had been a rather long one, and in a different direction from that which he usually took.

Mr Dottery sat quietly, like a child, and could not help being a little astonished at his own feelings as he sat there. For, instead of feeling that he had come to visit some poor crazed creature – an old woman who pretended to a higher knowledge than that of her tribe – he was conscious of seeing someone a little like himself.

But, throwing such thoughts out of his mind as mere nonsense, Mr Dottery looked more closely at Mrs Tubb.

Mrs Tubb was wrapped in a grey mantle that had, perhaps, seen better days, the hood of which was over her head. She appeared to be immensely interested in the fire, into which she cast now and again pieces of furze and dry heather, in order that the flames might blaze up, under a great pot that stood upon two iron bars, and threatened every moment to boil over.

Whenever Mrs Tubb cast in a piece of furze that crackled and flamed, she spoke in a low tone, as if to the fire, and Mr Dottery thought that she said these strange words:

'Most Reverend Father in God, we present unto you this godly and well-learned man.'

Mr Dottery doubted his own hearing, 'though perhaps,' he thought, 'the poor lonely woman was but, in the queer language of her cult, delivering an incantation that might raise the Devil.'

Mr Dottery felt cold.

The light of the fire died down. A few sparks only seemed to live, and shortly these would go out.

Suddenly the woman took up a bundle of furze that was in a corner and cast it upon the fire. Flames roared up the wide chimney, the pot boiled over, and Mrs Tubb stood before the two girls, who were trembling with fear.

They each held out a shilling.

As the woman took the money into her hand, Mr Dottery fancied that he heard her whisper, 'Not everyone that saith unto me, Lord, Lord, shall enter ...' but he could hear no more, for the two girls both exclaimed together with one voice, 'Which of us be to marry Tommy Toole?'

The woman, who, Mr Dottery thought, seemed to forget where she was, looked down upon them both and said distinctly, 'Secondly, it was ordained in order that the natural instincts and affections, implanted by God, should be hallowed and directed aright ...'

'Tommy Toole do know where his instincts do go,' laughed one of the girls.

'He will marry you both,' cried the witch.

'But where shall we live?' inquired the Spenke twins. 'In a pigsty, palace, or barn?'

'In a palace,' exclaimed Mrs Tubb joyfully.

The woman turned and hurried to the fire, where the pot boiled angrily, but, being come to the fire, she hesitated, as though she was not sure how to proceed. She stood for a moment as if she talked to the foaming and bubbling pot, and Mr Dottery, from his corner, thought that she said, 'He opened the rock of stone, and the waters flowed out: so that rivers ran in dry places.'

When the pot grew a little quieter, a knocking was heard at the door and, Mrs Tubb saying 'Come in', Lottie Truggin entered with the rice pudding.

No sooner did Mrs Tubb turn from the fire and perceive the pudding and take the dish into her hands, than she sat herself down with her knees apart and her cloak spread over them, and, taking a large dessert-spoon from her pocket, she began her meal. She was soon eating so eagerly that she did not notice Mr Spenke's daughters rise from their seat, go softly to the door, and let themselves out.

'I ought to have kept them here,' said Mrs Tubb, when she saw that they were gone, 'and then I might have spirited them away.'

'Not to a witches' sabbath, I trust,' said Mr Dottery.

'No, but to everyday labour,' said Mrs Tubb.

She finished the pudding.

'How was it made?' she asked Lottie excitedly.

Lottie told her, for sometimes she had been allowed to make a rice pudding for herself under the careful eye of Mrs Taste.

'You first wash the rice,' said Lottie, 'and then you butter the dish, and next you mix the rice with milk and white sugar, and shed a little nutmeg upon the top. Bake in a slow oven.'

Mrs Tubb clapped her hands.

'I believe I could make one,' she exclaimed, and handed the empty dish to Lottie.

'Aren't you going to wash it?' asked Lottie.

'Put it out in the rain,' replied Mrs Tubb.

Lottie took the basin, but without saying 'thank you' for it, and went out of the cottage a little pettishly, thinking that Mrs Tubb was a dirty old woman. Mr Dottery had watched with a surprised interest all that had happened. But, as soon as he was alone with the witch, he approached her with a shilling in his hand.

'Do you think it right,' asked Mr Dottery, handing the shilling to Mrs Tubb, 'that a bishop should marry?'

Mrs Tubb looked extremely distressed.

'I fear they cannot always help it,' she replied, and poked the fire with a burnt stick.

'I understand you,' said Mr Dottery.

'But why is Canon Dibben so interested in my affairs?' he asked.

'Because he wishes to save your soul,' replied Mrs Tubb.

Mr Dottery went to the door.

'We have one service a week at Tadnol,' he said, 'on each Sunday afternoon.'

'So I have heard,' said Mrs Tubb in an altered voice.

Mr Dottery opened the door and went out.

THE REVEREND Silas Dottery was not gone out more than a hundred yards into the November darkness before he perceived two burning lights approach Mrs Tubb's cottage from the Dodder direction. He paused to watch them. Evidently the great automobile, driven by the Devil, had come for Mrs Tubb.

Although not a nervous man, Mr Dottery, without noticing that he did so, hastened his steps and, giving little attention as to where he was going, he missed the path, taking another that led him out of the right way.

God is still a carpenter. It was not for nothing that He was received into the family of Joseph. He can dovetail events, He can measure time, He can cut out a plank, so that it exactly fits the roof where He wishes it to go. He can do more than that. He can turn sawdust into bread. He can take a rude and knotty log – such as John Bunyan was – and plane him away until He gets a smooth surface to write His will upon, yet is able to leave the hard knots below, for He was never one to spoil by Art the rough matter of Nature. God knows how to use a jack-plane.

Such a happening as the arrival of Mrs Tubb was not likely to escape the ears of Mrs Dibben, who knew well enough that Lottie Truggin, the merry, saucy, plump maid at the Tadnol Rectory, would wish to walk out upon the heath to visit the witch.

Lottie was watched. John Card, the Tadnol sweep, had been bribed by Canon Dibben to keep a look-out. A sweep is usually a man who likes money as much as a lord, and John Card saw no reason why he should not put a few shillings into his pocket, earned by his spying, and yet be no Judas to his spiritual pastor.

When Mrs Taste was making the rice pudding for Mrs Tubb, John Card had called at the Rectory to inquire whether the date had been fixed for him to bring all his tools with him in order to sweep the study chimney, that stood a daily and a nightly risk of catching fire.

But Mrs Taste shook her head.

'I would prefer not to mention the matter to Mr Dottery for a few days,' she said, 'for he may not yet be quite recovered from the thought of that awful journey.'

Mrs Taste put the pudding into the oven.

'Shadrach, Meshach, and Abednego would have been lucky had they discovered a pudding like that in their fiery furnace,' said John Card.

'They found God there,' said Mrs Taste. 'But Lottie is to carry the pudding to Mrs Tubb this afternoon.'

John Card had no chimney to sweep that day, and so he walked to Dodder and called at the Vicarage. Mrs Dibben heard his news eagerly. She decided what she must do, and began at once to make the necessary preparations. She sent out to the nearest farm for a fine fat chicken to cook for her husband, and she also ordered some apple fritters to be made – a dish that Mr Dibben loved.

A clergyman's study is often a penitentiary of the first order, and causes him who waits there to grow more hungry than an imprisoned harlot. And often, during the long hours of a dull morning, as Mr Dibben sat there, he would so long for the bell to call him to a meal that he could hardly remain still upon his chair. He had once almost wished that his wife's nose, that was so quick to smell out iniquity, would show a like cunning in the discovery of a few truffles for dinner.

As soon as ever a whiff of the roasting chicken crept into the study, Mr Dibben began to finger his pen as though it were a fork, hoping that the time would hurry, so that he might have his fists in the dish.

Canon Dibben was not disappointed. Seldom had he eaten so well, and though Mrs Dibben did her duty too, he took the larger share, and when that bird was taken out into the kitchen, the cook groaned woefully.

As a rule after lunch the Canon would rest for an hour in an easy-chair, smoke his pipe, and meditate over the immoral doings of the clergy and his neighbours. Sometimes he would look at a book.

Mrs Dibben wished to find him one now with pictures. She looked through a magazine of modern painting, but they would not do. And then she took down and put near to her husband, who seemed to doze, the illustrated adventures of *Gil Blas*, done in 1865.

Canon Dibben appeared to wake up; he took the book up in his hands and began to look at the illustrations. He also looked at the clock and seemed surprised that it was only three. Had it been ten at night he would have the better understood his wife's kindness.

However, when she saw that he had examined carefully all the pictures, Mrs Dibben came to him and said commandingly:

'My dear, this very afternoon you must really and truly discover what it is that Mr Dottery keeps in his study cupboard. You must go at once to the heath, where you will meet Lottie Truggin. There is a deep pit by the side of the road that resembles exactly the pit into which the brethren of Joseph put their younger brother. You must lay hold of

Lottie and throw her into the pit, and you must not let her go until she has told you the secret of Mr Dottery's wickedness.

'That's your duty to your neighbour. For it is quite impossible for me to persuade Julia Parsons to give up meeting Farmer Greedy after church, near the red barn – I have often told you what happens there – while all these dreadful stories are told of Mr Dottery. And how can I rightly admonish naughty Edith – who will watch the bees in Mr Johnson's garden – when I am told that a girl who wears only a hair-slide to cover her wickedness does dance upon the *Holy Bible* in Mr Dottery's study? Go at once and pluck the truth out of Lottie.'

Canon Dibben shut up *Gil Blas* and shook his head.

'I cannot do it,' he said, trembling violently.

'I know better,' replied Mrs Dibben, 'for I am quite sure that Lottie will tell you all when you are alone with her.'

'But how had I better begin?' asked Mr Dibben anxiously; 'what am I to do first?'

'Do as you did in the wood,' replied the lady; 'for unless I know soon what is hid in Mr Dottery's cupboard, I shall die.'

Canon Dibben breathed deeply. The odour of baked meats still scented the house. He rose heavily from his chair, turned into the hall, and took down his hat and overcoat. For some while he could not find the right armhole, but his wife helped him at last, and he went out.

22 LOTTIE THINKS IT'S THE DEVIL

MR DOTTERY was slightly bewildered. He had never, as far as he could recollect, been lost before. He felt it a little strange to be standing there upon the cold heath at that time in the evening.

Although he could not see the hour by his watch, he believed that it was past five o'clock. In his warm study at home the lamp would now be lit. Why was he not there, reading contentedly under its mild light? Often at tea-time he would read poetry. He remembered even then some lines from Young's 'Complaint': these he uttered aloud.

Bless'd be that hand divine, which gently laid
My heart at rest, beneath this humble shed.
The world's a stately bark, on dangerous seas,
Here, on a single plank, thrown safe ashore,
I hear the tumult of the distant throng,
As that of seas remote, or dying storms.
And meditate on scenes more silent still,
Pursue my theme, and fight the fear of death.

Mr Dottery wished, as he warily pursued his way, that he could remember a little more. But the 'Complaint' was at home. He raised his hand as if to take the volume from the bookcase. He knew where it was – in the second shelf – the cover being of gold and the date 1817.

Mrs Taste would now be coming in with his tea, together with a covered dish in which there had always been hot buttered toast. The tray always had a pleasant and a comfortable look – a pot of choice China tea, and sugar and cream.

Mr Dottery walked a little in one direction, and then a little in another. He wondered how many times he had turned round in the darkness. Perhaps he was even then facing Dodder. The idea made him feel uneasy; he had no wish to discover himself at the Vicarage there. He knew the black tea that Mrs Dibben brewed would do him no good.

Mr Dottery tried to recollect a map of the heath that he had once seen. There were roads marked that went this way and that, and also a deep pit. The heath was a wide place, and he might never get to Tadnol. He remembered that the extent of the heath had surprised him when he looked at the map. It was quite possible to continue walking there until you came to Portstown.

Mr Dottery began to consider the homing instinct. He believed that there were beasts, as well as birds – pigs, for instance – who always knew their way home. But how could he in that wilderness change himself into a pig? He must remain for ever only a poor man who had lost his way.

A gust of wind blew upon Mr Dottery. He remembered a character of Congreve's who inquired of a young lady in the London streets which way the wind blew. Mr Dottery wished he had taken more notice of this little matter before he went out – but, of course, the wind changed sometimes.

Mr Dottery walked a little way further, and then he stood still and listened. He stepped back hurriedly. He heard voices that seemed to come from just below his feet, from somewhere under the earth.

'You shouldn't have pulled me here,' a girl's voice said.

'I only wished to ask you a question,' a man answered.

'Ask your question, and let me go, for 'tis getting late,' said the girl, beginning to cry.

The man raised his voice: his tone was sacerdotal.

'My good child, know this,' he said, speaking as though from a reading-desk, 'that thou art not able to do these things of thyself.'

'I wish I had waited for Mr Dottery,' said the girl, sobbing. Her voice could now be easily recognised as Lottie Truggin's.

'Mr Dottery is safe at Tadnol,' said the man, who was certainly Canon Dibben. 'He is busy with a young woman, and has just asked her this question that I must ask you. How many parts are there in a sacrament?'

'Two,' replied Lottie: 'the outward visible sign and the inward spiritual grace.'

'Come, I will show you a mystery,' cried Canon Dibben.

Mr Dottery coughed.

'It's God Himself,' exclaimed Mr Dibben in terror.

'Or else 'tis the Devil,' said Lottie.

23   MR DOTTERY IS KIND TO LOTTIE

A MAN of wide reading is never surprised. No event can ever occur that he has not read of as happening in the past. Somewhere or other in books, whatever he sees or hears, he has read of before. Of all the many strange situations in which a man may be placed from that early day when Adam, being afraid himself to climb a little tree, bid Eve get the apple, nothing, however grotesque or absurd, of the many strange doings under the sun, has been omitted from the stories of mankind. Though many a censor has been busy, nothing has really been left out; all that has happened may be read of somewhere.

Mr Dottery smiled. He remembered that in *Don Quixote* the voices of Sancho and his Ass were heard as coming from under the ground, and so what could be more likely than that the voices of Canon Dibben and Lottie Truggin should come up too.

Mr Dottery noticed that the rain had ceased. He lowered his umbrella, and felt in front of him for the edge of the pit, out of which two persons were now climbing.

Canon Dibben was the first to appear, and stood, panting with his exertion, beside Mr Dottery. Mr Dottery shook him warmly by the hand, as if he had met him, which was not very likely – for Mr Dottery never attended such functions – at a ruridecanal meeting.

'The evening is growing a little dark,' observed Mr Dottery.

'Very dark, indeed,' replied Canon Dibben.

'I must confess, to my shame,' said Mr Dottery, 'that I have lost my way.'

'And I,' said Canon Dibben, 'have never found mine.'

123

Mr Dottery had always, quick and living in his mind, the first precept of religion – to forgive. Canon Dibben had tried to do him harm, perhaps deservedly, but harm all the same, and Mr Dottery wished in return to do him good.

'I should be extremely glad,' said Mr Dottery, who noticed that Mr Dibben seemed a little glum, 'to have the pleasure of your company at dinner on the first of December.'

'At what hour?' inquired Canon Dibben eagerly.

'At half-past seven,' answered Mr Dottery.

'My establishment,' said Mr Dottery, after a short silence, 'is only a bachelor's, otherwise I should make so bold as to invite your esteemed lady. But, as things are, I fear that I can only extend my hospitality to you yourself. I have only Mrs Taste to manage for me.'

'You forget me,' gasped Lottie, who had, after many struggles and backslidings, climbed out of the pit, and had heard a little of the conversation.

Mr Dottery shook Canon Dibben by the hand and bid him goodbye. The Canon walked away in the direction of Dodder. He walked quickly, having perhaps the very instinct that his neighbour had wished for; though he had lunched well, the cool air of the afternoon had made him hungry again. He feared that he might be late for tea, for how long he had been in the pit with Lottie he did not know. Yet he believed he had done his best to obey his wife, and that he ought to be given as a reward a good supper.

As soon as the Vicar of Dodder disappeared into the night, Lottie approached as near as she could to Mr Dottery without touching him.

'I be frightened,' she murmured, 'for most likely, now Mr Dibben be gone, the Devil will come up to find Mrs Tubb.'

'He has already taken her away with him,' said Mr Dottery.

'But I be still frightened,' sighed Lottie.

'Hold my arm,' said Mr Dottery, 'and nothing shall hurt you.'

Lottie did as she was told, and wiped her eyes with his sleeve.

'Don't 'ee tell Mrs Taste that we walked like this,' she said; 'for all Dodder do know as well as Tadnol that I do fancy a clergyman.'

'I am glad of it,' said Mr Dottery, 'for a well-behaved girl should always love the Church.'

Although Lottie held Mr Dottery's arm, it was she who guided him, for the clergyman was completely lost, but the maiden knew her way, and soon, after a little wandering, they were in the right track that led to Tadnol. Lottie clung close to Mr Dottery, who walked easily now that his wandering feet were on firm ground. Lottie could not keep silent for long.

'Though I be so fond of the clergy, I don't like that Mr Dibben,' observed Lottie.

'Neither do I,' said Mr Dottery absent-mindedly. He had bethought him of a passage in Homer that describes a dark night.

'Then why did you ask him to dinner?' inquired Lottie.

Mr Dottery gently tapped his companion's head with his umbrella.

'Who was it,' he asked her, 'who bid us do good to those who do evil to us?'

'No one who do live in Tadnol,' replied Lottie, laughing, 'nor in Dodder neither.'

'But One who lives in Heaven,' said Mr Dottery. 'How strange it is,' he observed, stopping suddenly in his walk, 'that His words of kindness should be so little understood, for His commandments are easy, and the fulfilment of them full of the greatest joy, so that it is impossible that anyone who has ever listened to Him should leave His loving paths to wander out amongst bushes and sharp briars.'

'How came you to wander so far, then?' asked Lottie pertly.

'Because I am not a good man,' replied Mr Dottery, deeply moved.

They were both silent. The night grew darker.

'I be so frightened,' murmured Lottie. 'But if thee did put 'ee's arm round me, I would feel better.'

Mr Dottery did as he was told. He strode along happily, glad that he was easing her fears.

His head was bowed as he walked. He knew that it was not Lottie alone who needed support in a dark night. Himself, yea, all humanity, needed the same kindness.

24　MR DOTTERY REMEMBERS ST PAUL

NEWS spreads in a village with the certain speed of the ripples of water when a stone is cast into a pond. There is no stopping it.

Even during the darkest evening, when every creature is safely housed, to each fireside an item of news will find a way. Who has told of it? The night wind, perhaps, has driven a loose straw to tap at every door with the story. In a dog's howl it may be told, or in the cry of a hooting owl. Or have the fallen and yellow leaves the power to tell tales?

When the usual time came for Mr Dottery to return to his tea, Mrs Taste looked anxiously at the hot buttered toast. Lottie, too, was out, and Mrs Taste was worried about her. The rice pudding had been all Lottie's idea, for the housekeeper hadn't been at all sure that Mrs Tubb liked puddings.

'Suppose that she doesn't, why, then she might be angry with Lottie for bringing her one, and in revenge change her into a mouse. A witch can do anything,' thought Mrs Taste.

She waited uneasily for another quarter of an hour, that seemed to her anxious mind to be but a minute, and then she went to the back door and called to Truggin, who was still in the tool-shed.

Truggin came readily. He wished to remind Mrs Taste that the barrel of beer that was kept in the cellar, to which he had ready access, was empty. He wished also to recommend a barrel of the same quality, in case Bishop Ashbourne called.

'Who be missing?' asked Truggin when, after mentioning the beer, he listened to what Mrs Taste said.

'The master,' replied Mrs Taste, who, being a good woman, did not fear to utter that word, 'and Lottie.'

'Be they two together?' inquired Mr Truggin.

Although Mrs Taste did not altogether like the tone in which Truggin asked his question, yet she replied readily that she hoped so. Truggin sat down upon a chair near to the fire; evidently the case required consideration.

Fear, as well as kindness, can live in a corner. For more than twenty years Mr Dottery had been in his study at five o'clock ready to take tea. Mrs Taste looked at the kitchen furniture for comfort. All things were as usual, the fire burned brightly, and yet trouble was in the air.

Mrs Taste peeped under the kitchen table. Perhaps she supposed a messenger from Death crouched there, who had come to tell her that Mr Dottery had fallen into a pit and was killed. Mrs Taste looked at the fire, the tea-kettle stopped singing.

Fear is an odd companion in a room. Simple things that have always behaved in a proper manner change their ways in his company. Mrs Taste looked at the kitchen clock.

A moment before it had been going, now it was stopped. A flat-iron upon the grate moved as though to ask what had happened.

Mrs Taste was a devout woman. Her happiness rested upon two strong pillars – God and Mr Dottery. She was not ashamed to pray, and now she prayed in her heart that her master might come home safe and well, and that a rather late tea would not spoil his appetite for dinner.

Truggin, seeing her lips move, said 'Amen.' He rose slowly, and warmed one hand at the fire.

"'Tis best to find out what be happened,' he said, and went out of the house.

To look for any living or dead thing pleases all men's imagination. Had the good shepherd who once lost a sheep lived at Tadnol, he would never have gone alone to the mountains, the whole village would have gone with him. The news that Truggin had to tell quickly went to the inn, to the farm, to the cottages, to the hollow elm tree, and to the churchyard. Very soon a dozen lanterns were forthcoming, while all who could left their warm firesides to walk out upon the heath, ready and eager to discover the worst.

Meanwhile Mr Dottery, still holding Lottie near to him, while she now and again uttered a little purring sound like a satisfied kitten, was come to the summit of the hill, where the heath road dipped down into Tadnol village.

Standing there, Mr Dottery saw, coming towards them, and already about halfway up the hill, a number of lights and heard a number of voices who were describing excitedly how one and all of them had, some time or other, found a dead man, stark and livid. Never was any conversation more full of incident, for all had seen death in some way or another, and the idea of what might be seen by so many lights made fiction real, and never had death seemed more to be the fact of the moment, or was expected with more willingness.

'No one haven't been found dead since silly Minnie were took out of river,' said Mr Croot.

'Oh, but you've forgot Saint Susanna,' said a girl's voice.

'She did live before the new bridge were made,' replied Croot, 'and so were drowned dead before I were born.'

The lights moved on.

Though Mr Dottery held the breathing body of a young girl so near to him, he was not thinking of her. He knew that he was conducting her home in a manner that seemed to content and please her, and there was an end of it for him.

But Lottie, who had been happy in the darkness, did not wish to be made ashamed by the lights. Her affection for the clergy was well known, but to have her love so truthfully shown in the full shine of Mr Spenke's lantern did not please her modest ideas of a proper decorum, and she wished very much that Mr Dottery would let her go.

'I bain't frightened now,' she said, giving a timid wriggle.

But Mr Dottery did not take his arm away; his thoughts were elsewhere. He was remembering that the Holy Apostle Paul had once observed that the law had a shadow, for, the night being misty, the lanterns cast enormous shadows, made out of the bodies and the limbs of their bearers, to the right and to the left.

The idea of the apostle pleased Mr Dottery.

'Let us consider one another to provoke unto love,' he said.

'Not now, please,' whispered Lottie.

Mr Dottery did not hear her.

'For it is not possible,' he continued, 'that the blood of bulls and goats should take away sins.'

'Let me go,' pleaded Lottie.

But Mr Dottery could only look at the lights, as though fascinated by them. He had made a journey that night, and knew not how far he had gone. He was now returning softly out of the darkness into the light. He was one who believed that forgiveness breeds kindness. He had forgiven Mr Dibben, and now the good people of Tadnol had come out to meet him. The whole population of Tadnol seemed to be there, and the lanterns formed a ring about Mr Dottery and the girl.

They stood thus for a moment until Mr Dottery released Lottie in order to find his purse, so that he might give a largesse to the company.

'But where is Lottie?' asked Mr Dottery, after handing a pound note to Truggin, for the benefit of his friends.

'She be vanished,' said Farmer Spenke, who carried the largest lantern.

Tommy Toole stepped forward.

'Here be Betty and Nellie,' he said, showing the twins, 'and I know they be women same as Lottie Truggin.'

'You can name them each now, Tommy,' observed Mr Dottery, as the lanterns escorted him to his home.

25 CANON DIBBEN IS TOLD TO TRY AGAIN

C ANON Dibben was not one to believe that prevention is better than cure. He knew that the Church must have her fees, but he trustfully hoped that, if the ill-deeds of Mr Dottery were brought to light, he would – being shamed in the sight of all men – repent of his sins and do better.

'The Bishop,' considered Mr Dibben, 'was too hasty to forgive, but he would not forgive so easily the second time. If the girl that Mr Dottery kept so carefully hidden – and who, when clothed, came out, as Mrs Dibben affirmed, in silks and satins – could but be brought to light, then he himself, being a step higher up in the Church than Mr Dottery, would be the one to give the proper rebuke, and Mr Dottery could not – for no one ever did – keep his sin hidden for ever.'

All village sins like to air themselves, and to be seen and spoken to. They become a real thing in conversation, and they like to be noticed. What could be more natural or proper than that Mr Dottery should keep a girl? She had been seen climbing a tree, she had been seen singing in the garden.

The Church always grows fat when a fine iniquity is discovered. Mr Dibben pleased himself – as he walked in the darkness along the heath towards Dodder – by thinking of this discovery.

He imagined the scene.

As soon as he was sure of the truth, he – the accuser – would stand in Mr Dottery's room and point with his hand to the open cupboard door, out of which would step the naughty young woman, showing the very garters that Mrs Dibben had told him of.

'And what would Mr Dottery, with all his money, look like then?' thought Mr Dibben. 'A convicted felon would be a gay fellow compared with him. He would hold his hands before his eyes, so that he might not see those wanton garters, that Mr Dibben, armed with a higher power, might stare at boldly. And then, with the girl sent out into the kitchen for Mrs Taste to deal with, he, Dibben, would tell Mr Dottery – using carefully prepared periods – how he had wronged Religion.'

Thinking thus and happily, Mr Dibben entered the Dodder Vicarage gate, and was soon in the parlour.

Mrs Dibben was sitting knitting in her chair. She was also counting up – not her stitches, but all those who lived near who she knew had committed mortal offences. She had counted thirty-two, weighing carefully each sin so that it bore down the balance, when her husband entered.

'Have you found it all out?' she asked him.

'I have made a beginning,' replied Mr Dibben. 'I discovered the girl just where you said she would be, and as you told me to do, so I did. I took hold of her and pulled her into the pit.'

'And what did you do then?' asked Mrs Dibben excitedly.

'As soon as I had regained my breath, for the descent was steep,' replied Mr Dibben, 'I examined her diligently in some parts of the Catechism.'

Mrs Dibben looked at him coldly.

'It ought to have been a goose,' she said, 'instead of a chicken.'

Mr Dibben tried to mend his story.

'I was on the point of pressing matters further,' he said, 'knowing that all I did was to the glory of God and to the lasting good of the Holy Catholic Church, when Mr Dottery discovered us.'

'Oh!' exclaimed Mrs Dibben, 'and what did he do?'

'He invited me to dinner,' answered the Canon.

Mrs Dibben looked up gladly.

'That will be our chance,' she cried. 'I know now just what you must do. After dinner Mr Dottery is sure to fall asleep – all bachelors do – then your chance will come. You must find Lottie, hold her tightly in your arms even if she struggles, and be sure you don't let her go this time until you have discovered all.'

Mr Dibben rubbed his chin; he looked at his wife uneasily.

'Suppose that this plan should fail,' he said; 'for how can I be sure that Mr Dottery will fall asleep? Would it not be better for me to go right into the study, open the cupboard, and see what is there?'

'You will not get the chance,' replied Mrs Dibben, 'for the dinner is sure to be taken in the dining-room, and when that is over – for you must remember that you will only be two men – you will both take your wine, sitting in the great easy-chairs.'

'But when am I to find Lottie?' asked Canon Dibben; 'for you know that I always like to do everything at the right time?'

'I have already told you,' replied Mrs Dibben. 'You must linger over your wine, and when Mr Dottery falls asleep, you must help yourself from the decanter. Lottie is only seventeen, and she is sure to be sent to bed early.'

Mr Dibben looked troubled.

'How can that help us?' he inquired.

'You must go to her bedroom,' said Mrs Dibben decidedly.

'But suppose I can't find it,' sighed the Canon.

'You are to suppose nothing but what I tell you,' answered Mrs Dibben, frowning. 'But if, through your folly, all fails again, I have another plan,' she said.

'What is it?' asked Canon Dibben.

'If,' said Mrs Dibben, 'Lottie Truggin will not tell you about the girl that Mr Dottery keeps for his horrid wickedness, I have thought of another way of discovering her. You must enter the study in disguise.'

'And then?' asked Mr Dibben.

'You must open the cupboard door yourself.'

'I will try Lottie first,' said Mr Dibben.

26   SOMETHING LEFT OUT

GOD writes His will upon the life of a man. But He does not always write clearly, and sometimes He leaves out a whole sentence. For a long while a man may think that he has read rightly what has been written, then he sees a blank space and wonders what God has meant by it. Something has been left out – something important.

On the whole Mr Dottery had found contentment at Tadnol, but his contentment had always been that of a patient scholar, who has learned all that he thought was proper to know from his books. God had meant that to be, and yet something was missing. Within the leaves of his books, and hidden away in their pages, Mr Dottery had now and again noticed something that always slipped out of his way, and disappeared.

He had read in Greek, in Latin, and in Hebrew. He had read much in other tongues too, and yet he knew that he had missed something – a parcel of wisdom that he had never found, some secret that he desired to know.

As year followed year – passing like cloud-shadows over a narrow sea – he had always hoped to discover what this secret was, hidden perhaps in some lost page of one of his authors. Had the page left his hand suddenly like the proof page and been blown upon a summer's day to the river, there to nestle in the loving lap of Saint Susanna?

Mr Dottery was growing old. Soon, he knew – but how soon he did not know – all secrets in heaven or earth would be alike to him; now was the time to learn what the secret was, or never. He did not doubt that the peace that had always reigned in his heart, as he read or meditated in solitude, was a true peace, but, of late, he had been aware of a curious movement within him to go out of doors.

But what did he wish to go out to see? Out of doors at Tadnol there were the beasts of the field, tall elm trees, Farmer Spenke's loud voice, a creaking inn signboard, and perhaps one or two scolding women. Pigs, ducks, women – Mr Dottery had never thought much of them.

But there might be odd corners in Tadnol where other things lived. If he waited all day in the hollow tree, he might hear whispers. If he stood upon the green for an hour something strange might happen to him. So many things of importance are hidden and wrapped up; no good thing is likely to be discovered at once and easily. Often that which is clear enough to be seen is never seen, until a man cares not whether it's seen or no.

Mr Dottery wished to make some kind of move in order to discover what God had written too faintly to be read, before it was too late.

His fears about his journey to Portstown, from which he had been so happily saved by Lottie Truggin, had awakened him strangely, so that he had looked more closely into his own doings, and was set a-wondering whether he ought not to go to school again to a new master.

He was well aware that the autumn, yea, the winter, of his life was come. He had already numbered his days, hoping to devote those that were left of them to the pleasant studies that even in his youth he had found to be more precious than gold and silver, and kinder than the love of women. But God had spoken to Lottie in no strange tongue, and he himself had seen Saint Susanna in the river, and she had looked like a living girl.

What were all the old books of the law that he had been buried in – ought he not to follow a kind lead, leave all that behind, and rise in a new gospel? Was there another language, other than those that he had studied so long? Another writing that he had not yet tried to interpret?

Could the first lonely step, that moves early in a village, or ever the winter's dawn kindles a dim light in the sky, tell a story, though lowly, yet as marvellous as any life written by Plutarch? Would the last pains of a dying horse, who thinks the night is come at noontide upon the bleak down – though 'tis but the darkness of death – show as noble a picture after a life of toil as can be found anywhere written of the death of a great king?

Can a flight of plover, when the gathering darkness of the evening has become a living thing, beat a poem with their wings, and write words upon the storm that only the man who walks under the hill knows the meaning of?

In his college days, Mr Dottery had been a tutor and had taught pupils. Now he wished to be taught himself. Perhaps someone at Tadnol might tell him how to read a book that he had so far not understood a word of. 'Twas almost a closed book to him. Those green valleys – and was not the river valley of Tadnol one of them? – can find a voice at times that can be understood by those who have learned their secret. The bare branches of the elm can love upon a clear winter's evening the cold moonlight. The holy heath, when a storm passeth over it, can pray and sing, and tell strange tales.

Mr Dottery wished to know if, in any lane or meadow, heath or down, there could happen sorrows and joys, the proud acceptance of calamity, or the willingness to drink a full cup of pleasure, that had been spoken of so often in the history of the world.

Could anything as great as the classic story be told of Tadnol?

MR DOTTERY walked in his garden. The evergreen trees wore their winter look; the mists from the river kept them very green. The air was pleasant, and many a late autumn scent moved in the garden to please a calm sadness that came with the season.

Mr Dottery paused for a moment beside a small path. This path led, he knew, to the hinder parts of the Rectory garden, where vegetables were grown and also pigs were kept.

Nothing in the world can be so adventurous as a scholar, when he wishes to learn any new thing, or a very old thing that is new to him.

But, even with an adventurous will, Mr Dottery hesitated before he set a foot in this path.

The back parts of the Rectory garden were sacred to Truggin; they were also possessed by the servants. Mr Dottery had never stepped in that direction in his life. He would as soon have walked into the Pope's parlour without an invitation as into his own back garden.

But it was now his business to find someone to teach him a new language, and he meant to be brave. And yet he hesitated. He blamed his pride. Was it this that kept him from the gravel paths that the servants used?

Or was it that the angel of decorum stood, with a broom instead of a sword, to guard all kitchen entrances?

Mr Dottery moved one foot a little way. A gentleman, he knew, is an oddity. As long as he is well fed in his own rooms he will remain in them, but, when he feels hungry, like Diogenes in the street, he will sometimes behave curiously.

BACK PARTS

Mr Dottery withdrew his foot. He was upon the point of turning, in order to employ the few minutes that remained before lunch in walking up and down the drive, and now and again plucking off with his fingers a green laurel leaf to squeeze out the scent, when suddenly a loud outcry came from the back garden.

'Pig be out, and be eating all they fine cabbages!'

Mr Dottery took the forbidden path and strode into the kitchen garden. There he found Lottie, who, as merry as could be, was chasing the pig that had grown so cunning that he had discovered a way, in spite of Truggin, to open the sty door for himself. Lottie picked up a stick to throw at the pig, and saw her master.

'Stop 'im,' she called; 'throw thee's hat at 'im. 'Twill get out into lane if 'e bain't stopped.'

Mr Dottery did what he could. He threw his hat, and soon found himself in a trench of celery shooing the pig, and then tumbling over a currant bush. The chase was exciting, but at last the creature was got into the sty and the door closed.

Lottie looked at Mr Dottery and laughed.

'I trust that I turned the pig to your satisfaction, Lottie,' he said, 'though I know that I am not so clever a herdsman as Daphnis, and yet with you another Chloe, I think I might learn. When the pig first dashed at me I thought I saw its tusks and almost withdrew from the battle, for a wound from a pig is often mortal, but I turned him at last.'

'You should have clapped your hands,' said Lottie, 'instead of waving them.'

'But the pig respected me,' said Mr Dottery proudly, 'and I made it run.'

'Yes,' said Lottie, looking up at him slyly, 'and that be about all that thee can do.'

Lottie jumped upon the sty wall, sat there idly, and regarded her master. She saw nothing strange in his being there, it appeared to her to be the most natural thing in the world. Of course any man – if he was a man, and knew that a pig was out – would help to drive the creature in, and after the chase, if there was a girl there, he would talk to her.

Lottie knew that her mouth was a pretty one and made to be kissed, that her hair was soft and pleasing, and that her body, supple and well-rounded, could not fail to give satisfaction to a good man. God, she knew, had spoken to her, and so why should not Mr Dottery?

She looked kindly upon him.

'I am an old man,' said Mr Dottery, 'and I know that I know nothing. Will you be so good as to teach me my lessons?'

Instead of thinking him a fool for saying so, Lottie supposed that he only spoke the plain truth. She knew that he had spent nearly all his life in reading. Evidently he had a great deal yet to learn. Upon the heath, when she was released from the pit, he had held her like a baby, but she supposed that he did not know how else to be kind. Perhaps no one had told him that she liked a clergyman. She now wished to show him that she did.

She looked at him seriously, and ceased to swing her legs.

She was thinking what she had better do with him. She frowned a little; she had taken a load upon her – the load of a man. She must try to understand him. He was her burden, and she had to carry him. If he turned out to be a little heavy for her, she wouldn't blame him for that.

Beside the pigsty, he was only the same curious being that she had often seen in the pulpit in church, when she wondered what his legs were doing. There was always a grand dignity about him there. But sometimes, when he gave out the last hymn, he would give too a sort of grunt, as if to say, 'Well, that's over, anyhow,' and Lottie was always aware then that he was a man, and that a wishing creature, called a girl, might still amuse him.

'But what be 'en thee do want to learn?' she asked of Mr Dottery.

'To love,' he replied.

Lottie pouted. 'You must begin at the beginning,' she said.

'The rudiments?' cried Mr Dottery. 'I will begin with "Mensa".'

'You cannot learn our ways in a minute,' said Lottie. ''Twill be only a kiss the first walking out, and it won't be that neither unless the night be dark.'

'I will put myself entirely in your hands,' replied Mr Dottery. 'I will behave as you tell me, for I long to return a little of the loving-kindness that I have found in Tadnol.'

Lottie looked from Mr Dottery to her own legs, but he was not regarding them. Lottie thought she understood.

'Of course they be only me weekday stockings,' she said to herself; 'only wait until Sunday do come,' and she ran indoors.

That same evening, after Lottie had done her work, that she did very merrily, she asked leave of Mrs Taste to visit her grandparents.

'Grandfather Truggin did wink at I from tool-house,' she said, 'which do always show that 'e have something to tell.'

'Yes, Lottie, you may go,' said Mrs Taste, but be sure you wear your thickest shoes, for the lanes are muddy.'

'They bain't so very bad,' replied Lottie, 'and thee be always worrying about me blessed feet.'

'Only for your good, Lottie,' said Mrs Taste.

Lottie ran upstairs. Mrs Taste's harmless words had made her feel naughty. She did not go at once to her home. Instead of doing so, she slipped on a white frock, ran out into the garden, and danced amongst the trees. She went out of the gate and a little way along the lane.

Near to the Rectory hedge a man crouched and watched her. She skipped past him, ran into the Rectory garden, crossed the lawn, and peeped into Mr Dottery's study window. She tapped gently; he did not hear her. He was deeply engaged with his book.

She tapped louder. Mr Dottery turned in his chair and looked at the window. He did not seem in the least surprised at seeing her. He only said 'Saint Susanna', and turned to his book again.

Lottie vanished. She slipped indoors and changed her frock. Soon she went out of the back door to visit her grandfather.

When Lottie reached her home, running in hurriedly, she found that the kitchen furniture had been moved. The high armchair that Sexton Truggin usually sat in had been carried from its place. The chair was set out like a judge's throne in the midst of the room, and in front of it there was a space for the prisoner. When Lottie entered Truggin said to his wife: 'Put thik maiden in front of I.'

When she was suitably placed, he looked at her sternly.

'I have something to say to 'ee,' he said, 'so stand where thee be put.'

Mrs Truggin retired to a small chair set in a corner. There she sat down and began to sew.

Lottie stood still; she was not a little awed by such grand preparations for a state trial, and wondered what her grandfather would say.

Sexton Truggin wished to light his pipe; he struck a match. The match went out. He struck another that burned well. He smoked and looked at Lottie.

'Some folk do fancy driving a pig,' he said.

'And some do like spying,' retorted Lottie.

'Thik Dibben be the one to hear,' remarked Truggin, 'for John Card do watch and carry.'

'And what if he does?' asked Lottie carelessly.

'I be afeard for master,' observed Truggin, 'for 'tis only the wicked who be careful of what they do. Yes,' said Truggin, looking sideways at a great cloud of smoke that he blew from his mouth, 'the wicked and all they who don't want to be buried, be careful never to be seen. They bain't never to be caught behind no haystack or beside a pigsty. The wicked be they who eat in secret, but a good man's doings be open to all, and thik good man be Mr Dottery.'

'I am his teacher,' said Lottie proudly.

Mr Truggin took his pipe out of his mouth, he looked into the bowl and shook his head.

'There be things,' he said slowly, 'that a maiden may teach a clergy-man, and there be things that she mayn't.'

'They Spenke girls do learn Tommy all,' replied Lottie.

Mr Truggin ruminated deeply. He looked up.

'What be a kiss?' he inquired of the ceiling.

'Nothing,' answered Lottie.

145

'And a tousling that do only tickle and tease 'ee?'

'Nothing,' replied Lottie.

Truggin's tone changed.

'But they manners bain't for always,' he said; 'a man do soon stop 'is tormenting, and do bide thoughtful; for a moment all be still, and then — '

''Tis best to laugh and run,' cried Lottie.

'Thee do know,' said Truggin grandly, 'and court be closed.'

❝ "THE Lord will have mercy – He will abundantly pardon."'

'Everlasting mercy is promised us here – a free gift from God, ready for the sinner. There are the words – "He will abundantly pardon." This is what we all require. Pardon, and most largely given. There is no slackness, no half-measure in God's giving, every sin will be taken away, for the Lord will have mercy upon us all.'

Mr Dottery laid down his pen. It was not often his custom to write his own sermons, for he believed that many a better man than he had given to the world thoughts more pious, and to be borrowed. But, thinking to try himself, he made a beginning, choosing, however, a rather unsuitable moment for such an unusual effort, since it was almost dinner-time.

He was just taking up the pen again, and was going to dip it into the ink to write the word "Mercy" when Mrs Taste knocked at the door, and being bidden to enter, said excitedly, 'The wine, sir!'

'Oh!' exclaimed Mr Dottery, pushing aside his sermon with a little more eagerness than was strictly proper. 'I should have thought of that before, for I believe that Canon Dibben dines here today.'

'He does indeed,' said Mrs Taste, 'and Truggin wishes to know whether you desire him to wait at table.'

'Once,' replied Mr Dottery, in a gloomy tone that properly expressed his horror at the crime, 'when Archdeacon Ford dined with me, Truggin poured him out port with his soup.'

'But the Archdeacon drank readily,' said Mrs Taste.

'Out of politeness to me,' observed Mr Dottery.

Mr Dottery stood up and smiled.

'The madeira and the claret are already upon the sideboard,' he said, 'and I will go at once into the cellar and bring up the port.'

Mr Dottery carried a tall silver candlestick, he descended the cellar steps with his usual care, for these steps were inclined to be rather damp and slippery.

But once down the stairs, Mr Dottery looked about him with great satisfaction. The Rectory cellars were large. In days gone by, when the Tadnol ploughlands were tilled by hands that had long rested from their labours, many a Tadnol priest had been merry in those Rectory vaults; and 'twas said of one that, fearing the happy effects of the wine might leave him did he climb the stairs, the good man drank another bottle as a health to a plump toad, and hanged himself by the neck to a beam.

Mr Dottery went softly to a bin where the spiders had been busy. He drew from thence two bottles of very old tawny port. These he carried carefully up the stairs.

Going into the dining-room, he decanted the bottles as carefully as he had carried them, enjoying the rich scent of the wine as it flowed.

After doing so, he withdrew again into the study and sat down in his chair before a large fire, wishing to prolong the minutes that might intervene between the fetching of the wine and the arrival of his guest.

Mr Dottery closed his eyes and meditated thankfully upon the exceeding pleasant delight that God gives to those who trust in His bounty.

But Mr Dottery had not long to wait before his peace was broken by a loud ring at the front-door bell. Mr Dibben had arrived in excellent time. His host received him in the study, where Mr Dibben took the nearest chair to the cupboard, but started up suddenly, for he thought he heard a rustle inside.

'You are not cold, Canon?' inquired Mr Dottery.

'Why, no,' replied Mr Dibben, edging a little nearer to the cupboard, and appearing to listen.

A bell rang. Mr Dibben jumped up.

'Yes, that's our dinner,' said Mr Dottery, smiling, and he conducted his guest into the dining-room.

Mr Dibben had used his longest stride to get to Tadnol. His wife might have driven him there in the little car that she possessed, but she told him that the walk would make him hungry.

And so it had, for the evening air upon the heath had blown freshly, and by the time Mr Dibben arrived at Mr Dottery's table, no clergyman – be he whom you will – could have been more ready to dine.

The dinner was a good one – clear soup, a fine turbot, two fat pheasants, tender veal cutlets done in rich brown gravy, a curious winecake, anchovies on toast. And for dessert, olives, a ripe pineapple, walnuts and burnt almonds. Plain country fare, but not to be despised.

When a gentleman – and especially one to whom holy orders have been given – is an-hungered, and is not well practised in the fine art of eating well and drinking better, he should, above all things, never omit to say a thankful grace when rich fare is spread out before him. Such a grace – and a Latin one is the most proper to God, who likes the sound of Latin words – will be a better aid to the guest at a feast than the best of stomachs and the strongest of heads.

When the company reached the table Mr Dottery stood silent for a moment with his head bowed, intending to invite Mr Dibben to ask a blessing. But, seeing that the Canon had already seated himself, Mr Dottery merely prayed in his heart that God would give to all those who were poor as He had given to him, and sat down too. Mr Dibben had said no grace.

In every bottle of wine, as is well known, there dwells a little angel and a little devil. It is they who change the taste of the wine in the different seasons, the angel giving to a bottle a generous flavour at Christmas time, while the devil does make a glass taste the merrier for his presence upon All Fools' Day. Always the angel gives to him who drinks pleasant thoughts and happiness, but the devil sometimes changes a forgetful man into a foolish beast. This secret of the cup the goddess Circe understood, but Mr Dibben was not aware of.

Whenever he drank a bottle of wine at home, the wine was so poor in quality that the angel always moped and the devil ran away. But Mr Dottery's wine was of another substance, and he who had not the wisdom to remember God with the first glass was not likely to think much about Him when he came to drink the last.

Being sat down to table, Mr Dibben's first act was to stretch out a hand in the direction of the wine, for, though at home he was used to the maid waiting at table upon grand occasions, yet he supposed that Mr Dottery – whose way of living could not be as well ordered as his own – would wait upon himself.

Seeing Mr Dibben's wish, Mr Dottery moved a reproachful finger; the decanter was taken up by another hand, and Mr Dibben's glass was filled by Sexton Truggin, who, dressed in a suit of convenient black, waited at table.

THE DINNER

Mr Dibben had eaten no tea that afternoon, for, by reason of that abstinence, he hoped to take a better toll of Mr Dottery's hospitality. He now ate and drank by turns. Mr Dottery was speaking about a matter that was of interest to himself, but it only made Mr Dibben the more thirsty.

Mr Dottery had been studying that morning the ancient customs of the courts of kings.

'We are told,' he said, 'in the Book of Esther, of the manners that were used in those early days in a Persian palace. What strange preparations, we read, were made here for the impure bed of a heathen. Every virgin must be six months purified with the oil of myrrh, and six other months perfumed with sweet odours, besides those special recipes that were allowed to each upon their own election.'

Canon Dibben pricked up his ears; his thoughts were stirred. Was it possible, he wondered, that a virgin was being prepared for him in such a manner? What was this myrrh out of which oil was made? Did it grow in a wood? There had been a pleasant smell about Miss Cockett after Lord Bullman's party. Had she been gathering myrrh?

Mr Dibben's thoughts were beginning to wander into paths that they had not often traversed. His brow was a little clouded, and he frowned slightly. He appeared to be considering a nice matter of Church doctrine, that had two interpretations, between which even the well-balanced judgment of a sober man could not be sure of the right. Mr Dibben hesitated, he finished his glass, he believed he knew all.

But it was not long before the wise teaching of the loving mother, the Church – that always advocates sobriety – left to its own nakedness the mind of Mr Dibben, and so the devil that he had swallowed, having no charm to check his doings, began to tease the little angel.

'This foolish tipsy Dibben,' observed the devil, twisting his own tail into knots, 'has a mind to be even yet more merry. In his heart he wishes himself King Xerxes. Mr Dottery's remarks have moved him sadly.'

'He only wants his wife, poor man,' said the little angel.

'Or a girl,' said the little devil, with a wink, speaking in a muffled tone out of the body of Mr Dibben.

When the gentlemen were ready to leave the table Mr Dibben rose a little awkwardly and fell over his chair. Mr Dottery rose too, and begged his guest to pardon him for having seats in a dining-room that got so easily in the way. He then guided the Canon's steps to a safe chair beside the fire.

No sooner was Mr Dibben seated than the wine-devil stirred within him the more naughtily, while the angel could only solace herself with the thought that such doings were none of her business.

Mr Dottery sat opposite to his guest, and thinking to entertain him in a more sober way than in telling him Bible stories, he began to speak of the days when he used to go out a-fishing, telling a tale of how he had once hooked a conger-eel as long as the boat's oar, and as fierce as a dragon.

But Mr Dibben hardly heard what he said, and only looked strangely at Mr Dottery, expecting that he would behave as his wife had told him all bachelors do after dinner, and fall asleep. While Mr Dibben was expecting this to happen, the little devil began to whisper to him, so that the words mingled with Mr Dibben's own thoughts.

THE DINNER

'Come,' he said, 'if the cause is good, all means are proper. The more that can be done with Lottie, the more truth will be discovered. You have only to throw her down, address yourself stoutly to the common business, like a brave churchman, fancy yourself in the wood, and all will come out.'

Mr Dibben waited impatiently, regarding Mr Dottery with looks of anger, for never had he seen anyone who appeared to be more awake than his host. At last Mr Dibben could stand the suspense no longer. He left his chair and wandered unsteadily about the room, as though he wished to find the door. Mr Dottery attended to his wishes, guided him out, and returned alone to his chair.

A sense of unutterable relief overcame Mr Dottery when he returned to the dining-room without his guest. He hoped that something might prevent Mr Dibben from returning too soon, and he lost himself again in those sweet thoughts that the arrival of Mr Dibben had broken into.

He felt, as he rested there, a holy peace descend upon him – a great kindness. A kindness that had given to the wine that he had drunk a willingness to soothe, and that gave to him who had drunk of it, a few moments at least of perfect tranquillity.

Mr Dottery gazed thoughtfully into the fire ...

N O man – if he be of the right kind – should ever be too inquisitive as to what goes on in his own house. He should never, if he himself be content and at peace, wonder what others are doing under his roof.

Even if the clatter of fire-buckets is heard, together with the screams of servants and other horrible outcries, a man of sense will move out of the way only when the smoke reaches his room.

Strange noises, indeed, did reach Mr Dottery, but he did not regard them. Why should he? He had dined well, his chair was comfortable, his thoughts were of God.

A loud rattle was certainly going on elsewhere. Someone was chasing someone else in the rooms above, but all that Mr Dottery could feel of it was a sense of gladness that his guest kept so long away.

For who would wish to be interrupted in the pleasing thoughts that occupied Mr Dottery's mind. He was considering – and had certainly proved the matter to his own satisfaction – that a good and truly virtuous life, a life deeply rooted in the love of God and kindness towards men, gave the best taste to a glass of cool wine; and what better reason for the living of a good life could be given?

Before Mr Dibben had retired, Mrs Taste had brought in the coffee, and Mr Dibben had drunk his off in one gulp, in order to get back the sooner to the wine. Mr Dottery drank his cup more slowly, but he now gently lifted the decanter and filled his glass with old tawny port, that he held between his eyes and the fire.

As he tasted the wine, he was aware of water falling drop by drop from the ceiling onto the hearthrug. At first Mr Dottery watched the water meditatively, allowing the steady drip to merge into his pleasant thoughts about happiness. But, the water coming the faster, it occurred to him that he ought to call Mrs Taste.

He did not do so at once, for he was in no hurry to rise and ring the bell, and so he continued for a while to watch the dripping of the water, noticing with interest how the damp spot upon the ceiling grew larger, and wondering how it was that the hearthrug could absorb so much without looking the worse for it.

At length he rang the bell.

Had Mr Dottery been an ordinary person, he would have started up with astonishment when Mrs Taste came into the room, for never had she appeared before in such a dreadful condition. Her cap, that she always wore so becomingly, was pulled to one side, her black dress was torn, and her hair was undone. Mr Dottery only looked at her wonderingly.

'There is,' he said quietly, 'a little water falling. I notice that it is coming from the ceiling and falling upon the rug; perhaps the roof of the house requires to be repaired. I think that a tile must be missing.'

Mrs Taste held up her hands in horror. 'Alas!' she cried, 'he must have broken into Lottie's bedroom and upset the water jug.'

'Then it isn't the roof,' said Mr Dottery, looking relieved.

Mr Dottery now looked at the door which Mrs Taste had left open, for, through the door and from the kitchen, sounds of spoken words were coming.

''Tis a corner thee be in now, Canon Dibben,' observed a voice that was certainly Truggin's. 'And 'tis a kindness to keep 'ee there.'

155

'I only wished to ask Lottie a question,' replied the Canon in a meek tone, 'so you need not hold up the warming-pan so threateningly.'

'A question!' replied Truggin; 'but there weren't no call to throw a maid down in passage and theeself on top of her in order to ask her a question, for thee bain't Elisha.'

'I only tried to get at her ear,' groaned the Canon very sadly.

Mr Dottery was slightly startled.

'He could not surely,' he wondered, 'have supposed that Lottie had the same idle fancies as Heliogabalus.'

'Thee went the wrong path for it,' Truggin was heard to remark.

Mr Dottery rose slowly with a sigh.

'I fear,' he said, 'that Canon Dibben has lost his way. He seems to have wandered into the kitchen. Would you be so kind, Mrs Taste, as to ask Truggin to show him the correct way to this room?'

''Tis best for thee to go,' said Truggin, when the message was delivered in the kitchen.

'Oh, but I'd much rather go to Lottie,' remarked the Canon.

'I have sent her to bed,' said Mrs Taste.

'The very place for me,' rejoined the Canon.

Truggin did not reply; he took Mr Dibben up in his arms and carried him into the dining-room, and placed him in an easy-chair beside the fire.

Mr Dottery welcomed him politely; such indeed was his usage of all guests who came to his house, whatever their behaviour, for Mr Dottery never allowed himself to think – no, not for one moment – that anyone invited to his house was not behaving as all men and women should, in modest fashion. If worthy enough to be invited there, anything that was spoken or done that was a little curious could easily be accounted for by a passing illness, and all should be forgiven.

'Holy Mr Herbert has wisely observed,' said Mr Dottery, 'that the wine in the bottle does not quench thirst,' and he poured out two glasses of port.

Mr Dibben drained his glass. He sat up stiffly in his chair.

'I want my wife,' he cried.

'Perhaps you had better go home,' suggested Mr Dottery.

But Canon Dibben only gazed at the fire, following with his eyes the flames that went up the chimney.

Mr Dottery regarded his guest with the greatest sympathy.

'Poor Dibben,' he murmured, 'he must suddenly have become aware of the fact that he has taken a foolish journey. All journeys are foolish, except the one that makes Truggin happy. And now after going so unwisely far, this poor man – like many another erring Christian – wishes to return to his woman. But someone must guide him to her.'

Mr Dottery opened the study door and called.

Mrs Taste heard his voice and came quickly.

'Truggin had better take the gentleman home,' he said.

'But Truggin is not here,' replied Mrs Taste. 'He only waited for supper, and then he went to his cottage.'

Mr Dottery and Mrs Taste both looked troubled.

'I fear that I must go myself,' he said wearily.

A sudden bang not far away can make a good man start as well as a bad. There was a loud knock at the front door that made Mr Dottery jump. Mrs Taste, also a little disquieted in her mind, moved back a few steps, while her master opened the door.

Outside in the moonlight there stood a woman. She was wrapped in a large cloak, and carried a heavy stick in her hand.

'I have called to see Canon Dibben,' she said; 'I went to Dodder Vicarage and was told to come here. I wish to ask him a question.'

'Why, it's Mrs Tubb,' cried Lottie, who had crept downstairs in her nightgown, to hear what was doing.

Mr Dottery looked very pleased.

'Perhaps you will not mind walking home with the gentleman, who is a little alarmed at the moon,' he asked the witch, 'but first you must drink a glass of wine.'

'Beer,' replied Mrs Tubb gladly.

There was something in her tone that caused Mr Dottery to look at her more carefully. But she merely appeared to be exactly what everyone called her – an old hag – and so he left her to Mrs Taste and returned to the dining-room.

He found Mr Dibben sound asleep.

30   MRS TUBB THINKS THE HEATH GOOD

THAT evil little devil who had entered into Mr Dibben with the wine that he had drunk has two ways of tormenting a victim. He at first heats him in the middle and then troubles him in the head. He starts him a-loving, and then he sets him a-hating.

Mr Dibben, not being practised in his ways, was no match for such inner doings. If the devil had been less active with him, he would have been more gentle with Lottie. He might even have sought her sorrowing, instead of rushing after her into every room, until he at last caught her in the passage, where he was pulled away from her by Truggin.

Sometimes it happens that the outward acts of a poor drunkard are misunderstood. If a sad tipsy one is lying in the dust and talking to the ground, he may really be only praying to God.

Once, when a sorry example of a mischief-maker, who had taken his bottle, was led away from a service conducted by John Wesley, by two pretty and justified girls, they expected to be beaten and sworn at, but returned later to the preacher to report that the merry sinner had only meant love. Wesley smiled and continued his sermon ...

Mr Dottery permitted Canon Dibben to sleep for two hours, and then he roused him.

Mr Dibben awoke in a very ill temper, and, as is usual in such a case, he began to search in his mind for someone to blame for the trouble that he had got himself into, and for the utter failure of the undertaking. Being really a good sort of man, he never blamed his wife, neither did he blame Mr Dottery – for a sinner should only be blamed by God – but he bethought him of Bishop Ashbourne and the Bishop's wife, Agnes.

After speaking for a few moments about the unusually mild weather, Mr Dottery said, 'Mrs Tubb has called here, and is obliged to return to Dodder tonight. Would you be so kind as to give this poor woman your protection in her journey, for the hour is late. She awaits your pleasure in the kitchen.'

Canon Dibben rose from his chair, looked at Mr Dottery a little reproachfully, but allowed himself to be conducted to the front door. Mrs Tubb was invited to come to him.

When once outside, Mr Dibben looked startled. He ran towards a thick laurel-bush.

'There she is,' he cried. 'I saw her in white; she ran in there,' and Mr Dibben brought back a leaf to show to Mr Dottery. 'I saw her distinctly, and I will catch her yet,' he exclaimed.

'It was only Daphne,' said Mrs Tubb.

But Dibben nodded knowingly, shook hands with Mr Dottery, and followed his companion out of the gate.

'I trust,' said Mr Dottery, when his guest was gone, and he was alone with Mrs Taste, 'that you found Mrs Tubb easy to entertain?'

'At first I thought her a dreadful witch,' replied Mrs Taste, watching her master lock the front door, 'for she knew all about Tadnol, and then I thought her a drunkard, for she drank seven glasses of beer.'

'The mystic number,' cried Mr Dottery.

'And, after that, I was sure she was a bishop, for she was able to expound to me the fifth verse of the twelfth chapter of First Corinthians, that I happened to be reading.'

"'And there are differences of administrations, but the same Lord,'" observed Mr Dottery.

'She discoursed upon the whole chapter,' said Mrs Taste, 'but the twenty-third, the twenty-fourth, and the twenty-fifth verses appeared to interest her the most.'

'Ah,' said Mr Dottery, '"the thorn in the flesh" – But I will go to bed ... '

Mrs Tubb did not walk fast, she even loitered, and, when once upon the heath, she stood still.

The beauty of the night reminded her of the question that she wished to ask. The heath appeared ghostly and mysterious under the moon.

'I wanted to ask you, Mr Dibben,' she said, 'how the next line begins that comes after these, for I have forgotten it.'

'Go to the Devil,' muttered Mr Dibben, a little ungraciously.

Mrs Tubb was not abashed.

'These are the lines that I can remember,' she said:

Leave me, O Love, which reachest but to dust,
And thou, my mind, aspire to higher things;

'What comes next?'

Canon Dibben was not listening to her. The words that she had uttered came to him as a mere witch's jumble. He turned aside a little out of the path, and, when behind a bush, the devil left him and ran back to the little angel.

Mrs Tubb, left alone, held up her hand gladly.

'I remember them myself,' she cried; 'the richness of the night has reminded me,' and Mrs Tubb repeated the lines:

Leave me, O Love, which reachest but to dust,
And thou, my mind, aspire to higher things;
Grow rich in that which never taketh rust:
Whatever fades, but fading pleasure brings.

'Well, I'm glad I remembered,' said Mrs Tubb, 'but I certainly expected that Canon Dibben would have known.'

She turned to her companion, who came back to her angrily.

'What's the use of a good man trying to help the Church?' he shouted, so loudly that the moon blushed.

'The Church' – Mr Dibben stamped his foot – 'what is the Church that everyone makes so much of? All the Church does is to make a man hungry, and then turns the very meat and wine in his belly into vexation and trouble. Who deceives a poor priest and makes him vomit? Who hoodwinks him? Who made the b... ' – Mrs Tubb coughed – 'Church? But we all know the Bishop' – Mrs Tubb started – 'and his women,' said Mr Dibben.

'Woman, please,' observed Mrs Tubb, 'for Bishop Ashbourne has only one wife.'

'He's after two more, anyhow,' called the Canon, who thought Mrs Tubb was deaf, 'for my wife tells me that he is trying to entice two girls from Tadnol, and for what purpose do you suppose?'

'To light the kitchen fire, of course,' replied Mrs Tubb readily.

'No,' said Mr Dibben, 'they are sent for to make the Bishop's bed.'

162

'The very thing they should do,' replied Mrs Tubb fervently, 'for I know myself what a worry those unruly feathers are – nothing but mountains and valleys, and I always hated Switzerland.'

For a while neither Mrs Tubb nor Mr Dibben spoke. Mrs Tubb seemed by her looks to be very much enjoying her night walk, and, for a woman, she strode over the heath with extreme ease. But presently she appeared to recollect something, and said eagerly, 'Do you think those girls will go to the Palace, Canon?'

'It is being talked about,' replied Mr Dibben, a little more quietly, 'though Mrs Spenke says that unless the Bishop can himself tell the difference between them, she will not let them go.'

'Surely that ought to be easy,' murmured Mrs Tubb, as though she were considering some deep problem.

No more was said. Canon Dibben walked along in a sulky manner, kicking the stones in the path, and he did not even notice that Mrs Tubb never left the road to turn to her own cottage.

When he reached his gate, he went in without saying good-night, and without seeming to see the lights of a large car that waited a little way down the lane.

SOMETIMES when one least expects it, a charnel breath from those low places where the dead are laid comes to a man.

He may be at his prayers, and well for him if he be! He may be at supper, raising a wine-cup to his lips. He may be sitting under a tree in his garden with his friends, when the cold breath creeps up to him out of the rushes in the valley, touches his forehead, and nestles near to his heart, which begins to beat strangely – knowing its own danger.

Such a breath – dark and sultry – came to Mr Dottery as he sat reading one afternoon beside his study fire. The flames, that a moment before had glowed brightly, now died down. The room became very cold, and Mr Dottery, in order to shake himself free from the strange fear that had come in to him, left his book and went out into the garden where Truggin had just felled a dead tree.

Mr Dottery found Truggin leaning upon his axe, and regarding the tree with a friendly and self-praising smile. He had been able to fell it, and his master had given him the wood.

Mr Dottery strode slowly to Truggin and asked him a question – a pertinent one – 'Will the tree live again?'

Truggin did not reply at once; it was necessary for him to think a little what the question meant before he answered it.

But soon he began to search about in the grass until he discovered a little ash shoot – for the tree was an ash – coming out of the ground.

'Yes,' said Truggin, ''twill live again, and the more fool 'e. Some folk bain't never content. For what could be better than to grow up in a large Rectory garden, to be struck dead by God, and then to be cut

down by Truggin? Tree be foolish, it wishes to root itself again.'
Truggin regarded the fallen tree with a grand contempt. "Tain't the
same wi' a man,' he said proudly, 'unless 'e be a big enough fool to
allow 'imself to go up a chimney in smoke. No, a wise man do know
that a well-digged grave is soon got ready, and 'e mid bide where 'e be
put for ever.'

Mr Dottery had his Bible before him. 'There is hope in a tree if it be
cut down,' he read.

'It is very right and proper' – the thought came to him, as it had
often come before – 'that a man should think and believe that he dies
eternally. Why should we think otherwise? Does goodness so wholly
dwell in us that we should consider ourselves an immortal home for
her sweet presence? Are we not built up – an edifice of clay, in which
there is scarce room for one wish that is beyond the folly of our days?
And cannot all our conceit be content with one desire only – to die in
the Lord?'

Mr Dottery laid his hands upon the Bible, so that his words might
the more deeply enter into his own soul.

'The end of man is ground,' he said sadly. 'It is impossible,' he pondered, 'not to think so at many times. For what right have we – who
dare not, even in our most lasting imagined hope, raise ourselves to
God's foot-stool – to think otherwise?

'But we do not,' considered Mr Dottery, smiling, 'leave at once and
utterly all that we have loved – a wine-bottle, buried with us, would be
well worth drinking in a hundred years' time, when we are but silent
bones. Why, indeed, should we have a less content to be buried than
worthy Truggin has to bury us? Is there anything worse to be found in

the darkness than we have seen in the light? And if, at the last, the loving hand of the Saviour do guide us no further than to a narrow hole in the nearest churchyard, what have we to complain of, so be it that He does guide us there?

'Will the Blessed Will be the less fulfilled, if He do but choose our grave for us, and walk that short journey to our last resting-place, as one that comforteth the mourners? What are we to expect – we who have broken every promise that we have made to Him? Dare we think that He should keep every promise that He has made to us?

'And those high mansions? Goes not simple Truggin very near to the truth of the divine love when he says the grave is the best of them? Does not the most blessed angel stand ever over us there to guard our sleep? Let the wild winds blow never so loudly above, they shall not disturb our holy slumbers. He that is the giver of good gifts will ever keep the best for the last.

'No charnel impurities can poison so sweet an unconsciousness as we will have there. How pleasant to rest for ever in a corner of the kind earth, fearing nothing, loving nothing, while above and about us, never lessening, never slackening for one moment its power of protection, is the peace of God that passeth understanding.'

'"For I know that thou wilt bring me to death, and to the house appointed to all living."'

Mr Dottery closed his Bible and went out again into the garden.

The winter sun that could be seen between the trees was setting amongst the dim reddened clouds over the heath. A blackbird uttered its strange, frightened cry in the churchyard. Something, the coming night, perhaps, had frightened it.

The sun – golden for a last moment – sank and was gone.

Mr Dottery walked as far as the drive gate. There he found Lottie Truggin in her black servant's frock, looking through the bars in order to try to see the village green.

'Have you nothing else to teach me, Lottie?' asked Mr Dottery, 'for since your first lesson beside the pigsty, I have learned nothing.'

'Oh!' cried Lottie eagerly, 'I want to know about they new people who be coming today, and Mrs Taste do say I mustn't go out because of my cold.'

'But you're out now, Lottie,' said Mr Dottery.

'Only peeping out,' she replied, with a sigh. 'And 'tis they people that I do want to hear about, but maybe thee'll go and see what furniture they have got. I do expect 'twill be a very small load, though 'tis said they be fond of animals.'

Lottie sneezed violently. Mr Dottery looked at her with compassion.

'Please go in, or else you will be ill,' he said, 'and I will go into the village and find out all that you wish to hear.'

MR DOTTERY opened the drive gate and went out into the lane. All was as usual there. The harvest from the elm trees was nearly all fallen, only a few yellow leaves yet remained to fall. Mr Dottery walked on until he reached the village green.

There it appeared to him that someone was expected, and although this was not the right time to move, yet sometimes changes would happen at wrong seasons – one leave and another come.

Beside the green two or three persons who belonged to Tadnol were looking anxiously towards the heath, as though something was expected to arrive from that quarter. One of those who looked was Mr Croot the blacksmith, and Mr Dottery inquired of him who it was that he expected to see.

'Farmer Spenke have parted wi' John Card,' replied Mr Croot, 'and 'tis a new man who be coming – an' here 'e be.'

Blacksmith Croot pointed to a wagon, loaded with furniture, that was slowly descending the hill. The wagon, one wheel of which dragged in a shoe, came slowly on, reached the bottom of the hill, where the wheel was released, and came to the green.

The horse was being led by Farmer Spenke, who had gone himself to Madder to fetch his new man. Amongst the furniture, and looking like a piece of it herself – for she was as old and withered as any antique table or chair – sat a woman, whose face might otherwise have been a contented one, except for a look of lasting fear. Though old, she had the startled and timorous look of a child who expects that at any moment a cruel stepmother will thrust her into a dark cupboard.

The man who sat beside her – old, too, but a hale enough fellow, with a great bushy beard – had the same look of troubled anxiety.

Between the two, and partly resting upon the knees of each, there was a cage containing two doves. The newcomer and his wife would look often at these birds with loving concern, as though they feared that the jolting of the wagon might trouble them.

Farmer Spenke unconcernedly led the horse to the house that John Card had vacated only that morning in an ill-temper, going, as all knew, to work for Mr Mere of Dodder.

As soon as the wagon stopped before the cottage, Mr Spenke, having brought his man there, took the horse from the wagon and retired. The man got down, and the woman, raising the cage very gently, gave it to her husband. He placed it within the cottage garden.

As soon as that was done, the man and the woman looked this way and that, fearfully, as persons will sometimes do who try to pretend that what they know must be somewhere near, is not there at all.

Mr Dottery, who had walked beside the wagon to the cottage, wondered what ailed the people. At last the woman sighed, as if a hidden fear that was in her heart had been eased a little.

'The bad road all the way from Madder have done they birds no hurt, I do hope,' she said timidly, 'but didn't we go by Tadnol Church and see they tombstones.'

'The doves are well enough now,' the man observed; 'and we may live many years yet.'

'What is your name?' asked Mr Dottery.

'Our name be Turtle,' answered the man, looking lovingly at the doves.

'Cannot I help you to unload your goods?' inquired Mr Dottery, who saw that only the bird-cage had been removed from the wagon.

'We left Madder, for we were afeard,' the man said, still gazing at the doves. 'In front of where we lived were those mounds, and no year did pass without two or three of they long holes being dug. And soon did come they who carry a corpse, that was to be put in under the dirt. And we could count another mound.'

Mr Turtle knelt down beside the wagon and touched the earth. ''Tis dark where the dead do lie,' he murmured. 'Only darkness be there.'

Even when they were unloading the wagon, Mr Turtle appeared to take no notice of Mr Dottery, and only when the last piece of furniture – a cracked basin – was carried into the cottage, did he look at his companion.

'And who be you?' he asked, with a look of horror. 'Who be thee's master?'

'I am an unworthy servant of God,' replied the clergyman.

Mr Turtle moved a little away.

'Thee do bury folk,' he said. 'Thee do stand and watch what do often stink, being put into the earth. No one don't never speak to the buried again. They leave their own door, never to return – 'tis that we fear.'

Mrs Turtle had not left the doves for one moment; she now carried the cage into the cottage, placed it upon the kitchen table, and, without thinking what she was doing, she lit three candles. Her husband hastily blew one of them out.

'Do thee know what 'ee have done?' he asked her. ''Tis three lighted candles that be put beside a coffin. 'Twill be cold death for we within a year. I do now hear the feet of they who have come to carry us out. 'Tis like the doings of a woman to bring death to we all.'

'Have 'ee looked up chimney, for 'tis cold for they doves wi' no fire in grate?' asked Mrs Turtle, wishing to change her husband's thoughts, 'and maybe John Card had no mind to leave cottage.'

Mr Turtle stooped down and looked up the wide chimney. ''Tis as thee expected,' he said. 'John Card never left Tadnol willingly.'

'What do you see?' asked Mr Dottery.

'All darkness where there should be a little light,' replied Turtle, going out into the wood-shed to fetch his rake. While he was gone, the doves began to coo happily; they were feeling warmer.

Returning in a moment or two, Turtle thrust the long rake up the chimney, hooked it into something, and brought down a great sack filled with wet rags.

''Twas well stopped up,' he said, and, in answer to Mr Dottery's look of inquiry, ''Tis what be done,' Mr Turtle explained, 'by folk who don't want to go.'

Mrs Turtle lit the fire and the smoke rose unhindered.

'The last time we moved,' she said, 'the Brines filled up the garden well wi' closet dung, and before that, when we went to Shelton, the Johnsons left a nest of wasps in cupboard under stairs, besides setting a block of wood over shed door that would fall if door were opened. But doves be hungry, 'tis time to feed they birds.'

Mrs Turtle unfastened the door of the cage; she took one of the doves, warmed it against her breast, then fed it with breadcrumbs out of her hand. Her husband fed the other in like manner.

They sat down at the table for tea. Though Mr Dottery was invited to join them, he did not do so, but only sat by the fire in one of the chairs that he had carried in, while the Turtles ate and drank in silence. They looked at one another fearfully, and now and again the man made an odd gesture with his hand, as if to frighten something that moved in the room away from where the doves were placed.

''Twas a pity we ever came away from Madder,' observed Mr Turtle, setting down his cup, and looking at the clock upon the mantelshelf that, for all its jolting, still ticked merrily, 'for time do go fast at Tadnol, whereas at Madder all hours went slow, and we know to where we be hurried.'

'Do thee mind our first fear?' he continued, speaking to his wife in a low tone; ''Twas when we went to church to be married. Thee did wear a hat wi' orange-blossoms, do 'ee mind that?'

'Oh, I bain't so forgetful,' Mrs Turtle answered.

'And all the time there were a mistake being made, for when we did come to church door, and I did pull out thik ring, expecting all to be in readiness, we did hear said in churchyard, though hidden from us, those terrible words – "Man that is born of woman hath but a short time to live, and is full of misery. He cometh up, and is cut down, like a flower; he fleeth as it were a shadow and never continueth in one stay."'

''Twas then that thee minded the goat,' said Mrs Turtle, 'for though to be married while a new grave were being filled in did mean that a haunting terror would torment all our days, yet thee did say that if we'd be kind to the poor goat and keep 'im alive we would live too.'

'And when the goat did die,' rejoined Mr Turtle, 'we did buy two geese to take our woes upon them.'

'True,' observed Mrs Turtle, 'and then we did begin to grow old. And so one harvest-time came, and we were out binding up the corn. Sun sank low over Madder Hill, and we heard the geese cry, but we knew not what had happened until we came home, and found that Squire's dogs had killed them.'

'And our fear came to we again,' said Mr Turtle, 'and we thought our time was come – 'twas when we worked for Farmer Hart – and all in a hurry we did buy they two doves.'

'Who do take our terrors,' whispered Mrs Turtle; 'but if anything do happen to they two birds, 'twill be our death too.'

'There be no hope in the grave,' said Mr Turtle. 'A dead body do lie there and crumble into dust. In that under darkness a man do rot away little by little. Slowly they small worms do eat 'is body, slowly they coffin boards do rot and let in the clay, and down there the man who once did boast of what he could do, be only the maker of one kind of dust. And that dust be the man.'

'But surely then,' said Mr Dottery, 'all our fears will be gone; and is that so entirely to be dreaded, which takes from us for ever what we have feared most?'

'We only know now that we fear, and then we shall know nothing,' replied Mr Turtle. ''Tis our living fear that we fear, and that do ever widen and grow, for no comfort can come to a man that must die.'

'But the doves,' said Mr Dottery, 'will not they die too, and they are not afraid? Consider how many boys and young girls have paid early their debt to Nature all uncomplaining. And our many sins, shall we not be glad to die and leave them behind us?'

''Tis hard that our evil ways, that be bad, should drive us to death, which be worse,' said Mr Turtle; 'for if evil torments here, how much more does our happiness, when we know that it only comes to be gone?'

'All true joys,' said Mr Dottery, 'ought to lead us kindly to the grave, for they have given us a foretaste of heaven.'

'And that heaven be but a wormy sodden bed,' observed Mr Turtle.

'No,' said Mr Dottery, 'it is eternity.'

'And what be that?' asked Turtle.

Mr Dottery was silent.

''Tis what I do fear,' said Mrs Turtle, with a shudder. 'For bain't we something now that do move and listen? In the early morning, doves do coo, and they loud village cocks do answer one another. Then the sounds of folk moving do begin, but soon we shall hear nothing, for, having lived, we shall live no more.'

'We had better have been born as the mud in the lanes,' moaned Mr Turtle, 'that in summer-time do change into dust that the children do play wi'. Were we thik mud, we'd never be put out of sight for ever.'

Mrs Turtle began to break up a few little sticks that her husband had brought in, together with his rake. She put these sticks into the fire one by one.

'I do go about the house,' she said, 'and touch what be ours, and Turtle do rise up early and go to his work. All the time I be at home, I do look to they doves, who do feed upon our fear, for when they go our fears will kill us.'

'Have you no children?' asked Mr Dottery of the woman.

'Oh, yes,' replied Mrs Turtle, 'but they don't come to see us now, for they say that we only heed the doves.'

'Is there no way, then, to rid yourselves of your fear of death?' asked Mr Dottery. 'Cannot you trust in God?'

''Tain't wise to put one's trust in a murderer,' replied Mr Turtle.

'But cannot you think more kindly of death?' asked Mr Dottery.

Mr Turtle shook his head.

33   WHAT IS LOVE?

LOTTIE TRUGGIN possessed a warm and simple heart; she liked old men, and she loved a clergyman. The clergyman that she loved was Silas Dottery.

Lottie had wished, ever since she was a mere babe, to have power over a man whom she could always laugh at. She had looked and learned. She knew that there was scarcely anything in a youth to excite laughter. A young boy was made too serious a creature for a girl to make fun of. A boy was never afraid, he would do boldly every deed that came in his way – good or bad – and in courage there is never anything to laugh at.

No brave young man, as Lottie well knew, could ever sin in his own eyes. He is always doing right. Lottie did not care for that kind of life; it was, to her, perfectly dull. To be led out to a field, and to be used with no scruple of conscience, to be just proceeded with as if one were a tree under the axe, what entertainment was there in that?

Lottie knew that young people have a right to do everything; she could do what she liked herself. But there are those, she also knew, who do a silly thing and not a right thing, in order to bring amusement into the world.

'And who can there be,' thought Lottie, 'better than a clergyman, to behave curiously?' A clergyman's ways, from the creation of the world, have been peculiar; his doings in bed, at prayers, or at meal-times should always make the home merry. Old men are afraid, Lottie knew, and the clergy are the most afraid; that is why they are always so amusing.

WHAT IS LOVE?

For a young girl to be amused by him, everything ought to be a sin to the man. To look at a green field with a few daisies in it should be a sin. To leave the study table and to walk out into the sunshine before he has completed his sermon must be, to a good clergyman, a sad crime. If he, only by an unlucky chance, looks upon a maid, he has sinned in every part of his body. To yield to the flesh, to touch or kiss a girl would mean many nights of unrestful repentance. For what kindly and lasting love can ever recompense such an injury?

A minister of the Gospel sees only as wickedness what a young man sees as a very proper performance. 'Tis all lust to a clergyman, he alone is the wrongdoer. There cannot possibly be any love in the matter at all, only filth and beastliness.

His wife, if he has one, came to him like a Bishop's licence to preach, or his first soft leather prayer-book. He would never dare to love her in the Vicarage summer-house ...

Lottie Truggin had peeped into church manners. Her grandfather had explained some of them to her; he had also told her that if a clergyman does wrong the church bells begin to ring of themselves. Lottie wished to hear them. In the old days she would have loved a holy abbot, but now she loved Mr Dottery.

The month of December, that can sometimes be a dragon, can, at other times, be a small mouse. It was like that now, windless, soft and warm. When Mr Dottery did not come home to tea – Truggin had told her where he was – Mrs Taste, forgetting for the moment all about Lottie's cold, asked her to run to the Turtles, and to tell Mr Dottery that tea was ready.

Lottie smiled; she was a young lady who made up her mind quickly,

177

and she at once decided what to do. Mrs Taste took down her Bible, Lottie ran upstairs for a moment, and then departed on her errand.

Tadnol was deserted when Mr Dottery left his new friends, for it was tea-time in the village, and everyone took their tea at the same hour. The evening was so pleasant and friendly that it might have made a match with a June night, and have done her no more hurt than a kind lover should.

Mr Dottery walked slowly. He was thinking of the Turtles, and was wondering if, in any way, he might take away their fear from them.

Coming along beside the green, he chanced to look up, and saw in the dim light the kneeling figure of a girl. Mr Dottery went to her. She wore a white garment, and her legs were bare.

She was Saint Susanna.

What man – be he ever so good – can hope to be always free from the temptations of the sinful flesh? Mr Dottery remembered the virgin saint. New stories had only recently been told about her. She had been seen, so it was said, even stepping out of his own study window, and skipping under the elm trees on her way to the river. He had himself once heard a tapping at the window, that must have been Susanna.

Mr Dottery recollected how he too had once seen her playing in the river. Since then he had often prayed that he might be permitted to see her again, not to drown her as the former rector had done, but only to ask her a simple question.

Mr Dottery knew that she sometimes came down from heaven to kneel upon the green. And now every moment that he looked at her, he feared that she might go back there again. Dare he catch her in his arms and hold her for a moment?

WHAT IS LOVE?

He now came quite near to her and remained looking upon her and delighting in her virgin graces. And then, without giving a thought to what he was doing, or what might be the consequence of such a sudden act, he leaned down and took her up in his arms. Instead of struggling, as it was always reported that she did the last time when she was so held, Saint Susanna nestled like a child against Mr Dottery's breast, and allowed herself to be carried along the lane, through the drive gate, and into the Rectory study, passing – as luck would have it – near to the green, John Card, who had walked to Tadnol, to inquire of the Turtles whether he might sweep their chimney for half a crown.

All angels and saints, as Mr Dottery knew – for he had often seen pictures of them in old books – though their garments might differ upon earth, wear, in heaven, the same cut of clothes. Saint Susanna was wrapped in a large white garment, just the kind of thing that he would have expected her to wear, though, had he looked closely, he might have been reminded of one of his own surplices. Susanna had covered her face, but left her legs bare.

Mr Dottery placed her in the great study chair, as gently as if she had been the queen of heaven, and regarded her with adoration, as became a Christian who had always honoured and revered the pious saints.

He knelt down upon the rug, and knew that there was no harm in so doing, for to honour and respect a saint as one would a king is right and proper.

'What can I do to be saved?' asked Mr Dottery, most humbly, 'saved from the fear of death, saved from my pride, saved from myself, saved from the terrible thought that the cruelty and suffering in the world is everlasting?'

'You must love me,' replied Saint Susanna.

'What is love?' asked Mr Dottery.

'At first it is looking,' replied Saint Susanna, 'after that it is wishing, and then it is touching.'

'But can I do all that at once, please?' inquired Mr Dottery. 'And how can I be sure that if I touch and embrace you, you will not vanish through the window and run to the river?'

'I will never do that again,' said Saint Susanna decidedly.

Mr Dottery looked at her and saw that she was laughing.

'Can I approach you when you make fun of me?' he said sadly.

Saint Susanna laughed the more. She jumped off the chair and ran to the door, then she waited a moment.

'What did they Turtles have?' she asked.

'A pair of doves and a cracked basin,' replied Mr Dottery, without giving any heed to what he said, for strange thoughts had come to him.

Saint Susanna opened the door and disappeared.

Mr Dottery was left alone in the study. He had held something in his arms that had been entirely new to him – a fancy, a delight, a rare sweetness, a strange shining bud, a little fabulous creature that slid away as soon as it was come.

When Mrs Taste brought in his tea, she found her master looking into the fire and considering deeply.

'Would you be so good, sir,' said Mrs Taste, when she had set down the tray with her usual care, 'as to exorcise a ghost?'

'Have you seen one?' asked Mr Dottery.

WHAT IS LOVE?

'Yes,' replied Mrs Taste. 'A moment ago a girl in white ran up the stairs.'

'Do not be alarmed,' replied Mr Dottery, 'that was only Saint Susanna.'

Mrs Taste moved the tray a little nearer to her master and withdrew.

34   RAW CURRANTS

'**M**Y son, despise not thou the chastening of the Lord, nor faint not when thou art rebuked by Him.'

Bishop Ashbourne repeated these words kneeling, as he took out from the kitchen oven a once large apple-dumpling that was now burnt to a cinder.

Rising and placing the unfortunate dish upon the table, the Bishop regarded an open book that was there too, with downcast eyes, seeing that as the cause of the trouble.

'If only,' he murmured, 'that other apple had looked the same – but alas, for us all!

Meanwhile the hour of noon drew on, and waked
An eager appetite, raised by the smell
So savoury of that fruit ...

'No,' he mused, 'Satan knew better than to cook that apple. And with her too, at the point of arriving.'

Bishop Ashbourne was right; his wife, who had been to the town stores to find fault with a pot of pickles, now came into the room. She looked scornfully at the ruined dumpling.

'Haven't you anything else for dinner?' she asked snappishly.

'Only raw currants,' replied the Bishop, reaching up to the mantelpiece, that was a little too high for him, and taking down a red paper bag.

'And Christmas coming, too,' said Mrs Ashbourne.

182

'I know it,' replied her husband mournfully, 'and never before have I contemplated that joyful season with so sad a heart. For never has it happened – except once, when I was a little boy and had the measles, with a rather high temperature – that the Holy Feast has come and gone without my dining upon turkey and plum-pudding, but, alas! I feel totally unequal to the task of cooking either.

'These currants,' said the Bishop, opening the bag and putting a few of them into his mouth, 'I purchased at the corner shop, that is a little way down Tubby's Lane. I foolishly thought, in the pride of my heart, that I would begin to gather, not the prayers of good men for Christ's Church, as I ought to have done, but the necessary and commonplace ingredients for a Christmas pudding.'

The Bishop hurried to a side-table, and opening a large book, he began eagerly to turn over the pages.

'That is not a cookery book,' said Mrs Ashbourne scornfully.

'It is Johnson's Dictionary,' answered her husband, 'and I am looking for "pudding".'

'And what does he say?' asked Mrs Ashbourne.

'That a pudding is,' replied her husband, '"a sort of food, or a gut."'

'How horrid!' exclaimed Mrs Ashbourne; 'but what am I to eat?'

Bishop Ashbourne cut the burnt dumpling in half.

'You see how it is,' he said, 'scorched to a cinder.'

'But have you had no success at Tadnol?' his wife asked him.

'None,' he replied, 'for Lottie Truggin will never leave Mr Dottery because she loves him.'

'What dreadful wickedness!' cried Mrs Ashbourne. 'But have we no hope of a servant?'

'There is only one chance,' replied the Bishop. 'For the other young women at Tadnol, who are free – the Spenke twins, Nellie and Betty – are willing to take service at the Palace, if the master – and, strange as the word sounds, they mean me – can tell them apart.'

'Wouldn't the mistress do as well?' asked Mrs Ashbourne.

'No,' replied the Bishop decidedly, 'these young women say that they must be known by a man.'

The Bishop looked down.

'And what else do the hussies say?' demanded the lady.

'That this knowledge can only be discovered in a corner, and that there is only one way of knowing them.'

'What is that?' asked Mrs Ashbourne shyly.

The Bishop looked at the burnt dumpling.

35   SCARLET AND HYSSOP

CANON Dibben believed that the leprosy of modern days was the sin of unchastity. He wished to change all men who use this sin, but first he believed his own urgent call was to cleanse the Church. He intended to begin with the Rector of Tadnol.

Mr Dibben had discovered a sure way – taken from the Scriptures – to cleanse the sinner. But also, he must of course expose the evil, and in order to do that he had cunningly devised a plan.

Whenever Mr Dibben bethought him of Mr Dottery's wickedness, he would always clench his hands and groan miserably, then he would relent a little and gently rub his knees. For, though the repulsive sin would make his zealous heart angry, yet in a little while he would see a repentant sinner.

And so Mr Dibben cunningly thought out his plan.

To face Mr Dottery with his own instrument of lewdness – the very wanton herself, the woman that he kept concealed – must be done by subtle means, and then he would proceed, right wisely using the formal ritual written in the law, to cleanse the sinner.

In order to be sure of the proper course to pursue, he read three times over the fourteenth chapter of the Book of Leviticus. After doing so, he visited John Card, knocking softly in a mysterious manner at the back door of the cottage, and arranged exactly what ought to be done in order to make a certain discovery. That day was Wednesday, on the Friday following – the 20th of December, his own birthday – Mr Dibben intended to make the attempt, but first he would sacrifice the bird, and early the next morning he would open Mr Dottery's cupboard.

'Such high doings, directed against the kingdom of darkness,' thought Mr Dibben, 'must surely reach the ears of Bishop Ashbourne, if not to the larger ears of Lord Bullman, for even the park railings of West Dodder Hall – raised high enough to keep the deer from jumping them – could hardly prevent a nobleman from knowing that Canon Dibben had unearthed a red-haired vixen from a hidden burrow.' To perform any act of righteousness such as that, in Mr Dibben's thoughts, needs of course a certain amount of prayer and preparation.

Mr Dibben prayed, and then considered what he must do. He felt it as a lucky circumstance and, in a small way, an answer to his prayer, that in the tiny little greenhouse at Dodder Vicarage, there grew a small plant of hyssop.

But that was not all. He had also to thank Providence that in his wife's wardrobe there was a scarlet petticoat, and upon her dressing-table a little cedar-wood box.

But even this was not everything that God did for Mr Dibben, who remembered noticing an earthen vessel, thrown upon the rubbish heap in the back garden. What could be more clear to him than that his plan must prosper. The running water would be the Tadnol river. The blood, the dead bird; the live bird, the cedar-wood, the scarlet and the hyssop, all placed in the earthen vessel, he would convey at the time he had arranged with John Card to Tadnol Rectory. And then, after the discovery was made and Mr Dottery's sin exposed to the light, he would sprinkle him seven times, and allow the live bird to fly out of the study window.

When an important event is soon to happen, the man who is the chief mover therein finds that his own excitement gives a prick to those lazy oxen – the hours – so that they move the quicker, and Friday soon came.

Mr Dibben had acquainted his wife with a part of his plan, how he was to discover the truth that was hidden in Mr Dottery's study, but he had considered that it would not be wise to tell her of the cleansing of the sinner, because he feared that she might have more than one objection to his carrying off the cedar, the hyssop and the scarlet that were necessary to this particular service – as a cross and prayer-book are to a service in Dodder Church.

Mr Dibben's hopes for the sinner seemed to be shared by the weather, for the mild winds that had pleased Tadnol all the autumn retained their warmth, even in the winter. And, indeed, though the end of our written story comes at Christmas, when a holier writing may be read in the skies, yet the same comfortable weather remained through all the dark days, bringing the primroses in February and the swallows in March, so that old Jacob Croot, who never went out at all, said that God and the Devil – whose quarrels cause all the trouble amongst the elements – must have become better friends.

As Mr Dibben stole silently out of his side gate, on the Friday afternoon, he was glad that the winter's evening was going to be so warm.

In one hand, and hidden under his cloak, he carried a knife, in the other a large earthen vessel.

His wife had not seen him go.

IF a man or a woman, or even a small child, has any particular fear, in a country place that fear is known to all.

Everyone knew in Tadnol that Blacksmith Croot was afraid of hornets. He had never seen one, but the idea that there were such insects made him nervous, and, when once he pricked a horse's foot with a nail, he observed that a strange sound of wings had frightened him.

Farmer Spenke feared a lawyer.

Mr Toole's mother kept her bed at the inn – though she might quite well have come downstairs – because she was afraid of tadpoles, and Tommy Toole had not made her fear of them the less by sometimes putting a few into her Sunday beer.

Even though Mr Dibben, with such an adventurous mind, had started off to accomplish so strange a service, yet at Tadnol no preparations were being made to receive him.

Sexton Truggin had come home to his wife, appearing to be a little out of spirits, for he had peeped into the hollow tree, where he hoped he might find a girl now that his hands were out of his pockets, but the hollow was empty.

As Mrs Truggin poured out his tea, wishing to enliven her husband, she said in a low tone that gave a greater guilt to the charge:

'They Turtles be afraid of a churchyard.'

Had Mrs Truggin said that a ship disliked the sea, or a lady her looking-glass, or that a young modern maid was afraid of love, she could not have given her husband a greater shock. His gloom left him, he pushed back his cup untasted.

''Tain't possible to believe,' he said, with unfeigned astonishment, staring hard at his wife, 'that anyone who do live at Tadnol do fear me pretty garden.'

''Tis true what I do say,' replied Mrs Truggin, 'for they Turtles do keep two birds that they do feed wi' their fear, and whoever do hint that they birds mid die, the Turtles do tremble, for they do fear to die too.'

''Tain't true,' exclaimed Truggin.

'I bain't no teller of lies,' answered Mrs Truggin, speaking very slowly. 'They two Turtles be afraid of being buried. They bain't moles. Nothing can be more awful to they two than to be lifted out of bed, wi' strange folk a-watching, put into coffins that do smell new, carried down they seven small stairs, taken to churchyard, and lowered by webbing ropes, that have to go too, into the gritty dirt.'

Mr Truggin said not a word. He reached for his cap, lit his lantern, opened – in a determined manner – the cottage door, and went out into the night. He passed the hollow tree. A Tadnol maiden – one of the Spenkes – peeped out from it and made signs to Truggin, and also pointed to herself.

Truggin saw her not: he hurried on.

A little later, he was noticed by Tommy Toole, who was out too, leading Mr and Mrs Turtle, with all the assurance of one who knows that he has the best of an argument before he opens his mouth, into the Tadnol churchyard.

Never king who owned a kingdom, the finest in the world, could have had so huge a pride in it as Truggin had in his charnel garden.

That favoured tree, the yew, and other evergreen shrubs, the grave-mounds, the paths – all these things sacred to blessed death – did Truggin care for with an exact and tender diligence. Outside the churchyard, Truggin was but an ordinary man, a little shrewder than most, perhaps, though never one to regard himself as superior to his neighbours – except when he buried them. Within the churchyard, Truggin was supreme. There Truggin would brook no rivalry.

Whoever came into Truggin's kingdom had to look to what he did. To leap a grave-mound, or to pluck a flower, would bring upon the offender so stern a rebuke, that he would quickly find another place for his thieving jollity.

But what roused Truggin's anger more than such mere naughtiness was when anyone hinted – however softly – that a trumpet might sound some day and the dead rise; for no good workman – such as Truggin was, or so learned in the full meaning of his mystery – could put up with, for one moment, such an idea of outrage and spoliation. To have so great a wholesome good given to man – a rich and so lasting a benefit – interrupted by a senseless sound, Truggin could never believe to be possible.

'Is God a thief?' he said to the Turtles. 'Is He a stealing Welshman that He should call up folks' bones from where they be laid? Where is the sense or reason in changing a man's clothes, who be well content with a suit of earth, soft as any flannel drawers? Who would wish to throw into a huge disorder the holy silence, and where be any content to equal the happiness of this pretty garden? All who do lie here do wish to stay for ever. Don't 'ee listen to none of thik foolish risen talk, don't 'ee never learn to look up. 'Tis best to look down for comfort, for when a perfect state be reached, what more need be said or done?'

THE DIRT OF GOD

The Turtles stood with bowed heads. They had never heard that kind of sermon before. It was as if someone was speaking, not to themselves, but to their fear.

'What Almighty God,' said Truggin angrily, 'would be so great an Ass as to break and disturb the only place in the wide firmament where peace do bide secure? Where earth do agree wi' earth, and dust wi' dust, and where no one do quarrel?'

Truggin paused for breath. The moon could be seen, showing dimly through the bare boughs of the great elm that grew beside the church-yard wall. The soft gloom of the warm, still night, together with a sweet, earthy scent, entered into the Turtles, so that they gently wept. Truggin noted their tears: they were proper to his garden.

'A thousand years of happiness can be found here in one moment,' he said, 'and though we do think to know be everything, not to know be the best. But what be there to be afraid of?'

Truggin bent down over a small heap of mould that was near to the wall, and picked up a little red worm.

'Look upon it,' he said, holding up the lantern that he carried, so that his guests might see the worm the better, 'there bain't no malice nor any hatred in a poor worm. 'Tain't no flea to bite, 'tain't no adder to sting, 'tis only the loving sister of they who do bide here.'

Mr Truggin put his lantern down beside the heap of mould. He let the worm go, and took up in his hand a little of the soil.

''Tain't earth that I do hold,' he said, ''tisn't earth at all, here be the dirt of God. There bain't no stone, no root of grass, no mould, that be man's here – 'tis God's. Our lively doings in the world are ours, here, our rottenness be God's. Do a dead man sin in the clay, do 'e wish to be a false witness, or to hurt or to kill, when 'e be buried? God don't bide wi' the wicked, 'E bain't happy in the rich, but 'E do bide content wi' the dead. Bain't a man easy whom the Almighty do cover and protect wi' His own body? You fear to die?'

Mr and Mrs Turtle bowed their heads lower to the earth.

'Thee do begin to die when thee be born. Life be only a death-bed, and our pulse do ring out our own passing bell, that do stop only when we be gone.

'Thee mid fancy, maybe, that the poor body of a man, ready for burial, be a sad sight to see, but 'tis then that 'is happiness do begin, and the winds do sing, and the smallest clod do whisper a word of gladness, when a man be taken out of sin into joy.'

Truggin took up lovingly another handful of earth.

'There be a river that master do tell of,' he observed, 'and if a man do but drink of its waters, all that he has ever been, all that he has ever done, be utterly forgotten. Below, in this pleasant garden, river do flow, this soil do sink into it, and men who do taste death here, do drink of its waters. A footfall do sound soft where God do kneel. Sounds come to they ears that be dead – a playing of music that only the dead can hear. In sorrow we sow our hours, in joy we reap what be good. Do thee fear to die now?'

The Turtles were silent.

''Tis proper for a tradesman to show his goods,' said Truggin, in a lighter vein. 'Come with me.'

The Turtles followed and Truggin led the way, treading carefully amongst the tombs. In a corner of the churchyard, where the grass was green and pleasant, there was a wide grave dug, that Truggin would show to the fearful, as a sample of his art. The grave was of the usual depth, as ordained by law, and at the bottom, Mr Truggin – with the forethought of a wise practitioner – had laid some clean straw.

Mr Truggin set down his lantern.

'The king in his palace,' he said, 'though 'e mid sleep by turns in each one of his three hundred beds, has none so good as this.'

Truggin descended into the grave and lay down upon the straw.

'No man,' he observed, 'need fear to die alone. During a little time, that be but a moment to him, all they that have known him in his life-time be laid down too. Or ever the cool earth do mingle wi' 'is bones, two generations will be gone. And above them all, the grass do show as green as when they lived. Bones do work upwards – soon a poor man do get near to the world again. And what be this earthy cover-ing? 'Tis only a fine lasting blanket that be tucked close, above which they little birds do twit and peck.

'Footfalls do pass, new folk do walk above, small rains fall soft, and the snowdrops do show. Winnie Croot do skip over Tadnol bridge. She be a little girl to have such quick legs, but she don't go no faster across river than a man do move from his coming to his going in his earthly pilgrimage. As a ploughman do stretch 'is eye over a furrow that hath no end, so do a man look who be dying.

'Life is a little matter, 'tis but a moment in a hollow tree wi' a naughty maid, 'tis now come, 'tis now gone.

'Thik be a wide and vast place,' said Truggin, climbing out of the grave and pointing back to it, 'though it do look so small. God, who do but lend 'Is love to the living, do give it to the dead for all time. There bain't no clod that do touch a bone that does not love with a greater love than the living do know of. And what be loneliness but to bide in our sorrows, for time bain't always kind?'

Truggin made a motion with his hand – a gesture inviting the Turtles to enter the grave.

They no longer looked into it with fear, and the goodman – as though it were incumbent upon him to take the first step – went down, taking notice of the earthy sides, as one would who looks at the walls of a pleasant room – an abiding place where one may hope to spend a long and restful night. Mrs Turtle, seeing him go so easily, followed down the steps, and they lay together at the bottom, Mr Truggin observing that this marriage-bed was one that no crowing cock disturbed.

'They silly folk,' said Truggin, 'who do talk of the raising of the dead, be the great doubters. They do not know God. Who would wish to give another tongue to a woman, and another greedy belly to a man, when once they be come here? Who are we to say that a little dead dust bain't as knowing – and more than as knowing – as a living man?

'Cannot He who made all the earth, wi' maidens to dance in 'en, make a little dust joyful too? And what be joy?' asked Truggin, sitting down upon the steps of the grave. 'Bain't joy only ease and comfort, a rest from our toil? What sense would there be in making a poor bone work again? We do know 'twould be easy for God to raise all up, but they two hands of His would be better employed in keeping all down.'

The Turtles lingered in the grave for a while, admiring the way it was made, then they arose out of the ground. They came up with no hurry in their steps. Their fear was gone.

Truggin leaned against the wall. He had nothing more to say. He had spoken he knew not what, but it was always like that when he walked in his garden.

The Turtles too remained silent. Their souls tasted the precious food of that place – the peace of the dead. They were conscious, as the dead there, of the sweet meditation of the dust, which, released of the burden of life, does know – though without thought – the joy of true content. The Turtles moved slowly away, leaving Truggin alone. They lingered a little under the yew, as if they longed even then to test the truth of Truggin's words and allow a thousand years – one loving moment there – to pass over them. They wished to die.

THE REVEREND Canon Dibben had unluckily forgotten an important detail of the adventure that he had undertaken. He now thought of it – the birds.

He stopped in the road, what should he do? He soon reassured himself. The Levite in the Bible had no doubt found it easy to catch two birds, and why should not he?

Mr Dibben remembered that when he was a little boy and the January snow lay upon the ground, he used to take the cinder sifter, raise it by means of a little forked stick, to which he tied a ball of string, and put crumbs underneath. Then he would creep away into the house, pass the string through the dining-room window – that was open a tiny crack – and wait for the birds to feed. Seeing them in the trap, he would pull the string, down would come the sieve, catching a bird or two. What could be easier than that?

But Mr Dibben was no longer a boy, he had grown older, though, if he could catch birds so simply then, surely he could catch them now?

Going down the lane into Tadnol, Mr Dibben was glad of one thing. He was glad that the Bible had not insisted upon his killing, over the running water, anything that was very fierce. A bird he might despatch, but a cat he could not kill. It was fortunate that the Bible understood his fears; he did not like being scratched.

Canon Dibben came into Tadnol village. The first birds that he saw were Farmer Spenke's ducks, who had wandered down to the river that afternoon, and were coming home late. These ducks were of a kind that are called runners. Mr Dibben chased them for half an hour –

he caught none of them. He grew warm in the hunt, though it occurred to him when he thought he had cornered the drake, that escaped him with a great flapping of wings, that neither Farmer Spenke nor his ducks might have read Bible stories.

Mr Dibben rested in the hedge near to where he had placed for safety the earthen jar. He watched the ducks walk into Farmer Spenke's yard. Mr Dibben permitted them to escape. Perhaps, according to the Jewish law, they were unclean. Mr Dibben thought not, and yet he was not sure. But there might be some other reason why they had not delivered themselves into his hand. Mr Dibben sighed. Ducks were birds, and he ought to have caught two of them.

'To obey the Bible, to do good to others,' he felt, 'is not easy.'

Mr Dibben left the hedge and took up the jar, that he fancied was now grown rather heavy. He wandered on, hoping to find a tamer bird than a duck. Looking into Mr Croot's cottage window, he saw a pair of canaries. Winnie Croot ran out of the door. Mr Dibben stopped her and asked whether he might take away those two canaries, kill one of them, and presently let the other go.

Winnie looked tearfully at Mr Dibben. She saw murder in his eyes, and fled screaming.

The evening was come, all the cottages had lights in their windows.

Mr Dibben hid himself behind an elm tree to consider what he had better do. A man he thought he knew by sight, who carried a lantern, entered a cottage. Presently he came out again, leading two others with him – a man and a woman.

Mr Dibben peeped into the house when the door opened. Upon the kitchen table there was a cage in which were two doves.

As soon as the occupiers were gone out of sight, Mr Dibben crossed the lane and tried the door of the cottage. The door was unlocked, and he went boldly in. He knew he was no thief; he believed he did what was right. What he took was as needful to him as the tribute in the mouth of the fish was to Saint Peter.

Mr Dibben strode towards the Tadnol river with the open pot in one hand and the cage of doves in the other. Had he met anyone he would not have been ashamed. Had he passed the Shelton policeman he would have told him his business, and explained to him all about the new leprosy that can only be cleansed in the olden manner, but he saw no one.

Canon Dibben crossed the Tadnol footbridge, and climbed a stile. He walked a little way down the river path that Mr Dottery had passed along when he first saw Saint Susanna. The moon gave him light and all things appeared to favour his design.

Mr Dibben had only walked a few yards when he noticed a railing that went across the river, that Mr Spenke had put up to prevent his cattle from straying. This railing was just what he wanted, for it was possible to stand upon the lower rail over the running water, without getting himself wet.

Mr Dibben softly set down the cage and searched for his knife. It was well that he did so, for his knife – a large one – had already cut a hole in his cloak.

Though a caged dove was an easier bird to catch than Mr Spenke's runner drake, yet Mr Dibben found even this task none too easy. He thrust his hand into the cage, and the doves pecked his fingers. Mr Dibben grabbed, the doves fluttered, and at last he drew one of them out. He was bold in a good cause. He held the dove firmly in one hand, together with the knife. With the other hand he guided himself along the lower rail, so that he might slaughter the bird over the running water. In order to do this both hands were needed.

He found, after one or two experiments, that he could balance himself by pressing against the upper rail and leaning over the water. Thus he had both his hands free.

Mr Dibben held the dove by the legs, he raised the knife, and struck at the bird's neck. He struck savagely and, had he hit the dove, he would certainly have killed her. But Mr Dibben missed his aim. The impetus of the blow caused his weight to press more than ever upon the rail that he leaned upon. The rail broke, and Mr Dibben fell into the water.

His first thought when he regained his feet – for the river was wide and shallow – was for the dove. Alas! he had opened his hands when he fell, and the dove and the knife were both gone.

Canon Dibben waded to the bank. Once there, he looked eagerly into the cage, expecting to find the second dove, but he had forgotten to close the cage door, and the other bird was gone too. He hoped they would both come back to him – they were both tame birds – and he waited a little, expecting them to return into the cage. He recollected putting a piece of cake into his pocket, as well as the knife. Before he left home he had crept into the pantry to steal them both. He now threw a little cake upon the grass and called to the doves. But no birds came.

Canon Dibben did not despair, he knew there is a reason for everything if one can only discover it. He had done his best, but no doubt he had fallen into the river, and the doves had escaped him, because the leprosy of Mr Dottery was too deeply rooted to be cleansed.

Mr Dibben walked away, carrying the empty cage. He began to shiver, and, fearing that he might take cold, he walked fast through Tadnol.

Leaving the cage by the cottage from whence he had taken the birds, Mr Dibben noticed a light in the bedroom window. He looked up and saw a woman leaning over the bed. He knew her by sight, she was the village nurse – Mrs Truggin.

38   BLESSED ARE THE DEAD

A LL unconcerned with the cleansing that he might soon have to undergo, Mr Dottery, sitting at his ease, finished his dinner. And, as was his wont at that hour – that should be one of the most happy in a country rectory that is well supplied with victuals and drink – Mr Dottery permitted his mind to enter the holy door of the temple of Sweet Melancholy.

Alas! there is no retirement in this world that is exempted from intrusion, and Mr Dottery's content soon forsook him, for when Mrs Taste brought in the coffee, she informed her master that a new sweep was to attack the study chimney, and, in consequence of his sooty proceedings, the room would not be in a proper state to be inhabited for nearly a whole day.

'Cannot you put the man off?' asked Mr Dottery, with a very deep sigh, 'for it is quite impossible for me to continue the life of Richard II – a king of England – unless I am surrounded by all my books.'

'I fear not,' replied Mrs Taste, 'for it is not John Card who is coming this time, but a friend of his who, he says, cannot be persuaded by any means in his power to come any other day than tomorrow. John Card himself is laid up at Dodder with lumbago, but, if he feels better, he hopes to call in order to see that his friend does his work properly.'

'I trust there is no doubt as to that,' observed Mr Dottery.

'I do not think so,' replied Mrs Taste, 'for John Card assured me, by a trusty messenger, that Mr Thomas can sweep a chimney as well as himself.'

'Can nothing be done,' groaned Mr Dottery, 'to keep this man away?'

'Nothing,' replied Mrs Taste, 'for one more fire in the study will be sure to catch the chimney alight, and as there is a large beam inside, the whole of the house will take fire, and we shall all of us be burnt to death.'

Mr Dottery tasted his coffee. 'Then I am,' he said, 'predestined to be made uncomfortable tomorrow.'

'And would you object, sir,' said Mrs Taste, who saw that her master had resigned himself to what must be, 'to our beginning to get the room ready tonight, for Mr Thomas is an early riser.'

'If the worst has to come,' said Mr Dottery, 'let it come now.'

'There is something else too,' said Mrs Taste hesitatingly, 'that you ought to be told of.'

'Let me hear it,' replied Mr Dottery.

''Tis said in the village,' continued Mrs Taste, 'that Farmer Spenke's new man, Turtle, be past hope of living, and that his wife do lie beside him, dying too.'

'God's will be done,' said Mr Dottery, 'but I fear, though they are but poor people, that the pangs of death will be very terrible to them. I know they fear it.'

'They do not fear death now,' said Mrs Taste, 'no, not so much as a gentleman would fear being moved out of one room into another.'

Mr Dottery turned to Mrs Taste a little quickly.

'Do the doves live?' he asked.

'No one knows what has become of them,' replied Mrs Taste. 'Some say that they have escaped, and some that Canon Dibben has stolen them, for he came through the village this very evening and asked Winnie Croot for her canaries.'

'And the Turtles are dying,' murmured Mr Dottery.

'As we all must,' said Mrs Taste.

Mr Dottery rose from his chair. 'I will visit them at once,' he said.

Mrs Taste helped her master in the hall to put on his greatcoat. Mr Dottery walked slowly down the lane. There was no mist now in the village, and the moon shone clear.

Mr Dottery's thoughts were sad. The Turtles were dying, and what had he done to ease their fears?

As Mr Dottery walked beside the green, he chanced to look up at the moon. Something dark – a shadow, a figure – passed over it. In the front room of the cottage where the Turtles lived was Mrs Truggin. She was putting things tidy, as the Shelton doctor was expected to come at any minute. She asked Mr Dottery to go upstairs.

In the tiny room above the Turtles lay in their bed; they did not look ill of any evil disease, but merely worn out, tired, ripe for death – and glad.

There was no mistaking their look, for each appeared to have one wish only, to die together.

'We be pleased they doves be gone,' murmured Mr Turtle. 'The cage was brought to us, the door be open, the birds be free. We be going too, for we have a mighty longing for death – thik corner where God be kindness.'

'I thought to find you troubled,' said Mr Dottery, 'but now I know that you have a right understanding, and that even your bones that are broken do rejoice.'

Mr Dottery knelt down and said, 'I heard a voice from heaven saying unto me, Write, From henceforth blessed are the dead which die in the Lord: even so, saith the spirit, for they rest from their labours.'

M R DOTTERY awoke early the next morning. He had fallen asleep, while gratefully considering how benignly death can come to those who have lost all fear of him. But, though Mr Dottery had slept peacefully, he awoke uneasily, for strange noises had broken into his slumbers from the room below.

At first he had been uncertain what the sounds were, for in the half-conscious twilight that comes between sleep and waking, little noises are often distorted and exaggerated. A slight sound enters the ear of the sleeper, that he fancies to be a roll of thunder, though it may only be Truggin outside talking to the pigs. The shutting of a door becomes the roar of a great gun, and the scamper of a mouse is a thief climbing through the pantry window.

Mr Dottery sat up in bed. The December light – always a loiterer – had hardly as yet shown its presence in his room. But though the light lingered yet in his own chamber, someone was about. Mr Dottery listened. Sounds came from his study – a clattering of the fender and fire-irons. Evidently someone was busy. Mr Thomas had come.

The sweeping of the study chimney was, of course, no new experience to Mr Dottery. He had once or twice each year heard John Card's brush ascending and carefully dislodging the soot as it went upwards. But now whoever was below appeared to bc unable to commence the task; Mr Dottery was made aware that the attempt was given over, and he heard a man's voice say loudly:

'The hour has come to discover the whore of Tadnol.'

Soon after hearing these strange words spoken, Mr Dottery

supposed that he heard someone give a tug at the cupboard door – and then there came a loud scream.

Mr Dottery hoped that no one was hurt. The study cupboard, he knew, was full of all his old fishing gear – nets, hooks, lines, and rods. He had pushed all in, thirty years before, having no regard to what went first, and only being glad that he could get the door to shut.

Mr Dottery rubbed his eyes, he wished to make sure that he was fully awake. There was no doubt of that, for a moment or two later Mrs Taste knocked at his door, bringing the hot water, and, as she drew the window curtains and arranged the towels, she observed – after she had bid her master good-morning – that there was a little matter below-stairs that needed his attention.

'But I fear,' she added, 'that the chimney is not yet swept.'

Mr Dottery groaned. Another day would have to pass before he could return to his happy labours. The groan that he uttered was replied to from below.

'What is that?' asked Mr Dottery.

'It's only Canon Dibben,' replied Mrs Taste, with a smile, 'whose wits have left him a little. Yesterday he tried to steal Winnie's singing-birds, and took the doves instead; today he came disguised as Mr Thomas, the Shelton sweep, and opened your cupboard door.'

'Alas!' cried Mr Dottery, 'I fear he is hooked.'

'He is indeed,' replied Mrs Taste, 'for, in trying to crawl out from under a net — '

'By Hephaestus,' exclaimed Mr Dottery, 'I trust that Lottie was not with him, for I am no Zeus to make a mock of such doings.'

'No one was with him,' answered Mrs Taste, 'but he might have crept out of the net had not a shark's hook caught hold of the seat of his trousers.'

'I will release him,' said Mr Dottery, with a slight yawn, 'as soon as I have dressed myself, read a little, and said my prayers.'

Mrs Taste quietly withdrew.

* * *

The large kitchen at Tadnol Rectory always gave a suitable welcome to any of his people who wished to ask the advice of Mr Dottery upon one subject or another – for there are often little perplexities that the friendly word of a just and good man can set to rights.

But it happened more often than not that the inquirer never reached the parlour, for a pleasant breakfast or supper, set out before a great fire, where the hostess was Mrs Taste, could not be left in a moment, and, by the time that he, or she, was well feasted, there often occurred a complete and utter forgetfulness of the reason for the call.

Upon the morning when Mr Dibben made his unlucky visit, the first kitchen arrival, who had a question to ask, was Tommy Toole, who came to say that his conscience – a busy accuser – had of late troubled him.

'I do not think that I ought,' he said to Mrs Taste, 'now that I am twenty-one years of age, to be always taking one or t'other of they young daughters of Farmer Spenke into hollow tree, or dark lanes, in order to find out the difference between them. I am punished now,' said Tommy with a deep sigh, 'for the girls say that they will only permit a bishop to find out about them.'

'And what do you wish to do, Tommy, now you are twenty-one?' asked Mrs Taste.

'I would like to marry,' replied Tommy.

'But which will 'ee have?' inquired Lottie, who was laying the kitchen table for breakfast.

Tommy Toole looked sadly at his boots, and did not reply.

There was a knock at the door, and John Card, who had completely recovered his health, appeared to finish the work that Mr Dibben had begun so badly.

'What was it,' asked Lottie of John Card, 'that Canon Dibben thought to find in study cupboard, as to be in such a hurry to get himself hooked?'

'He were looking,' replied Mr Card, with a knowing wink, 'for another bird.'

When one hears a scamper and a scuffle in a backyard, it is generally a dog chasing a cat, though sometimes it may be a human being who is run after.

Sounds of this nature were now being heard by those in the kitchen, and before Lottie had time to open the door to see what was happening, a gentleman, dressed in the highest cloth of his calling – a bishop's clothes – entered in a hurry, and being guided by his eyes and by his nose, stood at once at table and pronounced a blessing.

Mrs Taste was cooking sausages.

Bishop Ashbourne had hardly seated himself, before the two Spenke girls also appeared, flushed and heated.

'He did stop looking,' they both complained to Mrs Taste, 'before he knew which was which, for mother promised that we might go to the Palace as cook and housemaid, if he could call us by name. And who would have expected,' said the girl who might have been Betty, 'after all were arranged, that a bishop should hide in a tree?'

'And, when found,' said the other, 'should run so fast here.'

The Bishop looked nervously at the girls.

'Though I like turkey and plum-pudding,' he said, 'yet I set an even higher value upon the peace of my soul. But, at least,' he said, smiling, 'I did my best.'

'Why, 'e don't know skin from clothes,' said the Spenke twins.

'But I know my duty to God,' said the Bishop.

'And I do too,' exclaimed Lottie, and, putting her hands behind her, she repeated correctly the answer from the Catechism.

'A good girl,' said the Bishop, smiling at the well-cooked sausages that Mrs Taste placed upon the table.

Bishop Ashbourne had never been more at his ease, for though the Christmas turkey might never be forthcoming, yet with a good breakfast before him, and no sinner present who did not wish to be saved, he could forget for a moment the queer doings of more than one simple clergyman whom he had the guidance of – as well as the woman who guided him.

He had begun his second sausage with as good an appetite as he had ever had in his life, when Tommy Toole presented himself before the Bishop to ask a blessing. He pointed to the Spenke twins.

'May I marry one of them?' he asked. 'We will serve at the Palace.'

The Bishop blessed Tommy, and asked which he would have.

'Either one or t'other,' answered Tommy, 'so long as they both be dressed in wedding clothes.'

* * *

Mr Dottery dressed slowly. He had much in his mind to think of. There was Lottie, who loved him in her own odd way, and he wished to be kind to her too – in his. And there was also that kindness to consider that the Turtles had entered into.

After saying his prayer, Mr Dottery went to the window and looked out. The winter's morning had come into his garden; there had been a slight frost. The evergreen trees appeared at their best. A perfect stillness was everywhere, the tombs in the churchyard were whitened by the frost, and Mr Truggin, with bent back, was digging a new grave.

Mr Dottery left the window and opened his door. Upon the stairs he met Lottie; she looked troubled.

'Even though Canon Dibben do drink,' she said reproachfully, ''e be a clergyman, and great hook do hurt him sadly.'

'I hope not,' said Mr Dottery, and went at once to the study to release the wonderful fish. As soon as he had freed him, Mr Dottery said happily:

'I trust, Mr Dibben, that you will breakfast with me – there are fried soles.'

'I prefer toast,' said Mr Dibben angrily.

Major Works of T. F. Powys

Soliloquies of a Hermit (1918)

The Left Leg (1923)

Black Bryony (1923)

Mark Only (1924)

Mr Tasker's God's (1925)

Mockery Gap (1925)

Innocent Birds (1926)

Mr Weston's Good Wine (1927)

The House with the Echo (1928)

Fables (1929)

Kindness in a Corner (1930)

The White Paternoster (1930)

Unclay (1931)

The Two Thieves (1932)

Captain Patch (1935)

Bottle's Path (1946)

PUBLISHED POSTHUMOUSLY:

Rosie Plum (1966)

Father Adam (1990)

The Market Bell (1991)

Mock's Curse (1995)

The Sixpenny Strumpet (1997)

OF BIOGRAPHICAL INTEREST:

Cuckoo in the Powys Nest by Theodora Gay Scutt (2000)

T. F. Powys: Aspects of a Life by J. Lawrence Mitchell (2003)